The Survivor Program

Glenn Koerner

WestBow Press books may be ordered through booksellers or by contacting:

WestBow Press
A Division of Thomas Nelson
1663 Liberty Drive
Bloomington, IN 47403
www.westbowpress.com
1-(866) 928-1240

ISBN: 978-1-4497-3228-8 (sc)
ISBN: 978-1-4497-3229-5 (hc)
ISBN: 978-1-4497-3237-0 (e)

Library of Congress Control Number: 2011961174

Printed in the United States of America

WestBow Press rev. date: 12/14/2011

Contents

Chapter 1: Initialization

In the soulless depths of cyberspace, where endless columns and rows of ones and zeroes marched forth in their lifeless array of binary code, an unstoppable killer was brought forth. Ian Daniels leaned back from his computer and watched the code change without any outside instruction, in correspondence to the hypothetical scenarios he input. The program, adaptive in the extreme, used the vast knowledge it possessed to cope with any situation it encountered as if it were alive.

Ian fully knew the intentions of this project when he agreed to take the assignment. The program he wrote held fantastic possibilities if used correctly, but if used wrongly, the number of resulting deaths could be incalculable. He looked at the completed last line of code and envisioned the program taking on its full potential, wondering if he'd made a mistake. He'd been asked to do the insane, and with it now accomplished, it could never be undone. Only time offered the possibility of answering the question of whether he'd created a good thing or a monster.

He swiveled his chair around toward another computer console resting on the L-shaped desk and typed on the keyboard, accessing an external encrypted line between the classified location of the government research island and the United States. The computer room, bare of all furnishing except the computer desk and chair, had served as his office for the past two years while he was working on the program. No pictures or windows interrupted the monotonous, faded white of the walls as they boxed him in.

Ian liked having his work area empty, for it kept him free from distraction, but he did allow himself one diversion.

A temporary time lag occurred while waiting for the connection to go through. When the computer screen lit up, it displayed a lovely woman in her early forties. Her thick, dark brown hair tumbled past her shoulders in large round curls like unwound spools of ribbon. The woman's eyes never failed to catch Ian's attention. A striking shade of blue-gray, the eyes sparkled with golden flecks near the center of the irises.

"Hey, honey," she said softly with a loving smile. "How's the project going?"

"I input the new sequences," Ian told her. "It works, Jennifer."

"Really?" she asked. "Does this mean you'll be coming home soon? Our five-year anniversary is coming up, and I thought the project might make you miss it."

"Never," Ian promised. "Depending on how well the testing phases go, I could be home in two or three months. It's plenty of time."

Ian placed his hand on the monitor screen to caress his wife's face. Jennifer's hand reached up and touched the screen from her side, as if the surface of the monitor existed as the only barrier between them.

"I hope everything works out," she told him. "See you soon. I love you."

"I love you too," Ian replied. "Bye."

He switched off the computer link and downloaded his completed work onto a portable drive. As thin as a paperback book, the small black drive offered tremendous storage capacity in a form that was easily transferred between workstations around the facility. Even with the large amounts of data volume, the portable unit barely held sufficient room for the expansive survivor program he'd written.

Ian left the workstation, taking the drive with him. Heading toward the exit, he caught a glimpse of himself in the reflective metal of the door. He brushed his blond hair back into place and straightened the wrinkled black T-shirt that he'd worn since yesterday. So engrossed by his work, Ian had neglected to change clothes or shave. He scratched the stubble of his beard and decided it best to get cleaned up before announcing the completion of his part of the project.

When he slid his access card through a reader installed in the door frame, the metal partition blocking his way slid back into a recessed compartment within the wall. Leaving his work room, Ian walked down the reinforced concrete hallway to his room. Beams of metal in wide horseshoe shapes provided additional support along the ceiling and walls every ten feet and gave the military base a futuristic look. Situated underground, the facility's overhead lights stayed bright any time of the day or night. Lacking the ability to see the sun rising or setting allowed Ian to work without being distracted by the knowledge of passing hours.

Typing the code security gave him when he first took the job, Ian waited a brief moment while the computer inside the keypad beside his door verified the numbers. A small LED light above the keypad switched from red to green an instant before his room door slid back into the wall. Stepping inside, he pressed a switch on the interior door frame to slide the door closed again.

In the underground research facility, space came at a premium, so his quarters served his needs, if not his comfort. A bed on the left side of the room and a shallow clothes closet consumed the majority of the open space, leaving a narrow walkway to the washroom. No room existed for any additional furnishings, and as a military research base, quarters were for rest and changing between assignments, not for being at ease.

Setting the drive down on the bed, he entered the washroom. A toilet and cramped shower sat on either side of a small sink. The minuscule amount of available room engendered feelings of claustrophobia, but Ian forced himself to ignore it. He shaved the untidy beard growing on his face and turned on the shower.

After cleaning up, he left the bathroom and opened his closet, evaluating his choices of apparel. Colored T-shirts and plain jeans composed the bulk of his clothing options. When working on one of his projects, he shut down to the world, and looking fashionable became more irrelevant than he already believed it to be. Shrugging into a red shirt and navy blue jeans, Ian put on his well-worn sneakers and grabbed the portable drive on his way out the door. Because of his habit of working through the night, only the late shift security personnel were awake, but Ian wanted to test his program. He headed for the lab.

A wall of dark metal plates covered in straight rows of gleaming steel rivets near their edges blocked the entire corridor. Only three openings presented themselves in the heavy fortification. In the center of the wall stood a doorway, but thick, steel bars crossed it horizontally and kept people from passing through. The other two openings in the barricaded defense held mounted turrets of heavy-caliber machine guns manned by guards on the other side of the wall. A pair of soldiers on Ian's side raised their guns the moment he entered their sight, and the wall mounted weapons swung in his direction.

"Halt," ordered one of the guards.

Ian did as ordered and calmly waited for them to carefully examine the laminated pass card clipped to his collar. Security at the facility stayed ironclad at all times. Covered in layers of black ballistic armor, complete with helmets and face shields, the security teams running the checkpoints looked ready to hold off an all-out assault on the facility and not simply monitor those who came and went through the corridors.

"Cleared," the guard said after a moment of consideration. Even though they'd seen him numerous times before, the guards were never relaxed in their attitude toward him. They knew it only took one slip to compromise security and destroy everything, so they maintained constant and unwavering dedication.

One of the guards behind the wall touched a palm scanner, and the steel bars blocking the doorway slid back and out of the way. Ian stepped carefully through, and the bars closed behind him. Once he passed the security guards, he maintained an even pace and didn't make any sudden moves because Ian knew the soldiers watched him and would respond if he did anything of a suspicious nature. Ian passed through two more checkpoints before reaching the lab.

A second numerical access code, different from the one for his room, gained him entry into the primary research area. Bright white overhead lights flickered momentarily before turning on automatically when he came in, illuminating the lab in stark detail. Workbenches covered in tools, tangled heaps of colored wires, circuit chip piles, and magnifying lamps on long swing arms clustered in the center of the room. Digital readouts on wall computer banks showed graphs with changing progress lines as they received information from other systems. Lights blinked on and off, and gauges fluctuated as new data constantly streamed in. Ian took a screwdriver off one of the work tables in passing.

An eight-foot-wide window of reinforced glass filled the wall opposite the door Ian entered through. A stairway to the right of the sizable window led down into the holding area that was nicknamed "the hole" by the techs who worked in the lab. Bolted to the rough concrete wall of the stairwell, a bronze plaque held the raised lettering of the project, SHARA. The name *SHARA* meant Specialized Humanoid Adaptive Robotic Assassin. Ian's thoughts drifted back again to the unanswered question about his role in this project. Helping a robotic assassin survive dangerous covert operations in the place of humans seemed good, but whether someone might one day use the droid for unethical purposes gave him pause because his survival program would make the droid unstoppable.

Taking from the latest designs, the SHARA android was the most advanced unit ever built. Assembly and routine testing finished last month. Plans for additional features and upgrades concerned other departments not connected with Ian, but all of it would be for nothing if the droid couldn't survive dangerous missions in hostile territory. Ian's job revolved around creating a program to aid the droid in prevailing in what amounted to suicide missions. The completed program resided on the portable drive he carried.

Going down the ten steps into the hole, Ian observed the SHARA droid. Lying on its back at a forty-five-degree angle, the gun-metal-colored robot reclined on the only piece of furniture in the empty room. The diagnostic table under the droid supported it in a partially upright position, but controls on the side of the table allowed its motors and gears to ease the droid either down flat or fully upright according to the needs of the technicians. Ian turned a dial on the table's side horizontal and flipped a toggle switch. A soft hum emanated from the motors as they lowered the droid down.

Setting the drive on the table next to the machine's head, Ian found himself studying SHARA. Although he'd seen it before, Ian never bothered to examine the thing. As the project neared completion, he began thinking about it more and more. The potential applications of the droid, and possible misuse, were recurring thoughts in his mind of late.

Humanoid and vaguely feminine in shape, Ian thought it looked like a woman in a technological suit of armor plate. A row of upward pointing triangular sensors encircled the droid's upper cranium and increased the vision ability beyond the use of only its eyes. No lids covered the colorless mechanical eyes, and their crystalline gaze looked at the ceiling with an empty and dead stare. Microphones installed in shallow pits on the sides of its head took the place of ears, and a speaker hidden within the skull faced grin of its mouth replicated a voice for it to speak.

Using the screwdriver he'd appropriated, Ian took out the screws holding down a central plate on the robot's midsection and ribs. Lifting the plate out of the way, Ian got a good look at its internal structure. Reinforced metal bones supported its armored exterior skin while a jumble of technology made its home within the interior framework. A fist sized plastic box held the central processor, acting for all intents and purposes as its brain.

An empty slot waited between the central processor and the primary data drives. Ian slid the portable unit he held into the available space, and connectors on its exterior housing clicked softly as it locked into place. With the new drive installed, Ian reached for the first of three switches situated above the processors. Because each switch controlled some of the primary functions, they were all secured by a hinged cover, preventing the switches from being thrown accidentally. Ian pinched the sides of the first cover and released the front edge. The rectangular lid lifted up and back from a silver toggle switch.

When he threw the first switch, LED lights flickered as the interior systems powered up and came online. Flipping back the cover, he pushed the second switch into the on position and activated the central processor and secondary components. The clear eyes eerily swiveled in his direction as the droid became aware of him. Ian noticed the lifeless and unblinking stare centered on him and tried his best not to be unsettled by it.

"Good morning SHARA," Ian said, trying to shake the unease he felt. Raising the final cover, he flipped the last switch to enable primary motor function.

SHARA sat up, swung her legs over the side of the table and grabbed Ian by the throat. Lifting him off the ground, she pinned him against the wall with one hand. The skull like jaw opened for her to speak, but it didn't move with the words she said. SHARA's jaw hung open while the sounds emanated from the vocal speaker inside her mouth.

"You're attempting to interfere with my internal components," SHARA said in an overly synthesized voice.

"Negative," Ian choked out. "I installed the new program to aid your survival. I'm not a threat. I'm trying to help you, and I can't do that if I'm dead."

SHARA released him and returned to sit on the table. Ian coughed and gasped for breath. He looked toward the droid, but she remained motionless as if nothing had happened.

"You weren't programmed to attack me," Ian said finally. The droid turned its empty gaze toward him again.

"I must survive," she replied without emotion or inflection.

"What does it have to do with you attacking me?" Ian insisted.

"You removed the cover plate over my processor," SHARA answered. "You represented a potential threat to my unprotected circuits. My survival required the threat removed."

"Why didn't you kill me?" Ian hesitantly asked.

"You were only a potential threat," SHARA stated flatly. "Had you proved an actual threat or not explained yourself, I would've killed you."

Ian swallowed hard. SHARA's design intended adaptability, but the program he installed raised it to a ridiculous new level. He wondered if he'd be able to run any tests without getting himself done in while trying.

"I need to run some tests to see if the program interfaced properly with all your systems," Ian said. "May I proceed?"

"You may," SHARA answered.

Ian carefully approached the sitting droid. Reaching inside the open chest panel to activate an internal diagnostic, Ian felt like he was putting his hands between the spring loaded teeth of a bear trap. Any slight touch of the wrong thing, and he'd be dead in an instant.

"You appear troubled," SHARA observed.

Ian flinched at the unexpected statement.

"W-what makes you think so," Ian asked, trying to sound casual.

"Your heart rate and breathing have increased," SHARA explained. "And, your actions lack the efficiency they possessed in the previous times you've added programming to my systems."

"Humans have their own program," he told her. "It's called survival instincts, and it involves not getting near someone who previously tried to strangle you."

"I didn't try," SHARA corrected. "If I had tried, I would've succeeded."

"Nevertheless," Ian continued. "It makes me nervous to be in such proximity as your recent actions preoccupy my thoughts."

"You need not be nervous," SHARA informed him. "Your survival programming will keep me functioning in the face of many threats otherwise lethal. Any errors or program conflicts would endanger my survival. Your inspection of my systems aids, not hinders, my continued existence. Proceed."

SHARA's voice contained no emotions or changes in tone, but Ian understood he'd just been given a command. Refusing to follow such an order might be seen as a threat, so Ian quickly got back to work. He activated a remote sensor relay and stepped back.

"Follow me," he told SHARA and went up the stairs to the observation window looking down from the lab.

SHARA went with him, but her footsteps on the concrete offered up no sound whatsoever, and it raised the hairs on the back of Ian's neck thinking about being followed by a killing machine as silent as death itself. He tried desperately to ignore it and focus on the computer console in front of him. Located under the observation window, the console displayed numerous screens of data and control pads on its touch sensitive surface. The system interfaced with all the computers in the lab, and any of them could be controlled from this central point.

"This is a readout of your primary systems," Ian explained. He wanted everything he did to be in the open and as non-threatening as he could manage. He dragged his finger across the screen, sending the systems diagnostic window sliding away. Touching a small icon along the top of the console, he pulled it down and tapped it twice. The icon expanded into a window split into a dozen sections. Each division displayed a visual from SHARA's sensors or eyes. "We can monitor everything from here. We'll see what you see and can make adjustments as needed. Other programs available through the console let us keep tabs on your internal systems."

"Why?" SHARA asked.

"We must know if anything needs correcting," Ian answered. He activated another of the icons along the top of the screen. "See here? This tells about your cover plate being open. If ever you get damaged on a mission we'll be alerted and have all necessary equipment and replacement parts ready when you return, or we can outfit you on location."

Discussing the particulars of the project focused Ian's mind and allowed him to forget some of his nervousness.

"As soon as everyone else is awake," Ian explained, "we'll begin the first phase of testing."

"Testing for what?" SHARA asked.

"These sensors report no immediate conflicts in your internal systems or programming," Ian replied, watching the indicator lights on the left of the console turn green. "Further testing lets us observe how well your program adapts. We wouldn't want to send you on a dangerous assignment only to discover a glitch. Testing here lets us find and eliminate any flaws or oversights before they endanger you."

"I must survive," SHARA stated.

"When we complete these tests, you will," Ian assured her. "Everything checks out good. Let's get your cover plate reinstalled."

Ian and SHARA returned to the holding room, and SHARA sat down on the diagnostic table, waiting motionless while Ian closed and secured the cover plate. Tightening the last of the screws, Ian finished, but SHARA suddenly laid down and became as immobile as a mannequin. Ian wanted to ask the reason, but the lab door slid open, and General Williams, the head of the SHARA project, walked in.

Standard military camouflage fatigues and black boots composed the General's attire frequently, and today proved no different. The General kept his graying brown hair cut short to the point of being nothing but fuzz on the top of his scalp. Hard muscles showed through his fatigues, and an equally hard expression dwelled on his face as he looked at Ian from the observation window.

"Mr. Daniels," General Williams said in greeting. "I wouldn't have expected to see you up this early."

Although the General's words appeared pleasant, the condescending tone indicated otherwise. Since joining the project, Ian had never managed to get along with the General. Williams seemed tolerant of Ian only because Ian's programming formed the core of the whole undertaking. If the survivor program failed to do the job, everything else here served no purpose, but if the General could've accomplished his goals without Ian, he would've. The General didn't dislike Ian in particular. As far as Ian saw it, the General detested everyone equally and only put up with them while they proved useful to his own ends.

"I finished the program this morning," Ian explained to the General. "I came down to install it and run a few preliminary tests."

"Good. I'll wake the technicians," Williams replied. He muttered on his way out the door. "It's about time."

"He doesn't like you," SHARA observed, rising back to a sitting position on the table.

"I don't think there's anyone he does like," Ian replied. When an odd thought crossed his mind, he decided to ask SHARA about it. "Why did you lie down and pretend to be off when the General came in?"

"My databanks refer to one such as yourself who helps and assists another without the requirement of personal gain as a friend," SHARA stated. "Everyone else here has yet to be classified, so their threat level is currently an unknown. Until determined, it's prudent for everyone to be as unaware of me as possible. My sensors detected the approach of the General in the corridor."

"Wait a minute," Ian said. "You referred to me as friend."

"Correct," SHARA replied. "Your actions in assisting the testing of this project and your initial programming provides me with a greater probability of survival. You helped me and asked for nothing in return. Isn't this how you define friendship?"

"I suppose," Ian admitted.

Their conversation ended abruptly when three techs in white lab coats walked in. They set about their work of running through the operations software and checking internal relay connections in the main lab. When everything responded as ready, they signaled to Ian from the observation window.

"Stand up," Ian instructed.

SHARA obeyed without question. Ian unrolled a small map he pulled from his pocket. He indicated a location when he held it up in front of SHARA.

"We're here in the holding room," Ian explained. He drew his finger across the map to a large square room. "This is the training area. Report to the training area and await further orders."

SHARA's clear and lifeless eyes scanned the map before she began walking away. Up the stairs, past the techs, and out the door, she continued steadily along. The technicians had seen SHARA in action before during initial construction and testing, so her behavior didn't startle them. Ian wondered how they'd react knowing what he knew about SHARA and her new capabilities.

Chapter 2: Unexpected Deviations

Ian picked up a few tools from the center workbenches in the lab and slipped them into his pocket before following along with SHARA to input codes in door keypads and show his badge at security checkpoints. The techs remained behind, monitoring the sensor data on their computers. One of them pressed a button for the intercom system.

"SHARA droid en route to testing area," the tech said into a microphone. "All primary staff, report to positions."

Researchers and support personnel only recently awakened raced through the halls in a flurry of activity. The security checkpoints slowed them down in reaching their duty stations, but they made haste when possible. Monitors and sensor display screens activated throughout the facility with all information being recorded because the data gathered during the different phases of testing determined the course of the project and at what speed they should proceed.

"When we reach the first checkpoint," Ian instructed SHARA as he caught up with her. "Don't harm the guards. They have weapons, but they're only there for security. They won't harm you if you don't provoke them. They're not a threat. Understood?"

"Affirmative," SHARA replied.

Ian held his breath when they approached the checkpoint, but SHARA followed her instructions perfectly and waited for the guards to process them through. He sighed in relief when they made it beyond the military barricades.

"You are troubled again," SHARA observed without looking in his direction.

"Although you said you understood what I told you, I didn't know for sure how you would respond when the guards pointed their guns in our direction," Ian admitted. "If there was a programming error, it could've ended badly for the guards."

Ian stopped in front of a large round hatch leading into the testing area. SHARA approached and turned the wheel crank in the center of the door, pulling back the latches around its circumference holding it closed. With an effortless push, SHARA opened the heavy steel door and entered the next room. Ian followed her inside.

The training room impressed Ian every time he saw it. Countless trees filled the underground chamber, turning it into a lush jungle with thick leaves, low hanging vines crisscrossing between branches, and a carpet of ferns covering the rich soil. Lamps overhead simulated daylight enough for the plants' needs, and a sprinkler system provided artificial rain to keep the greenery well watered. Boulders cut from the island around the facility created variations in terrain, and a water pipe formed a river flowing through the center of the room. If not for the ceiling visible thirty feet above his head, Ian might've believed the forest to be in the wild and not inside a government facility under the earth.

SHARA remained motionless. Having already scanned the area, she took no further notice of it while waiting for instructions as ordered. When Ian reached to remove a panel on her upper right arm, she stepped away from him.

"It's alright," he promised. "I'm going to cut the BC-5 and BC-6 wires."

"Active power relays through those wires," SHARA stated. "Cutting them would cause sparks every time they contacted the metal of my exterior casing. It would also give away my position and threaten survival."

"You have no enemies in the testing area," Ian said. To make his point, he leaned against the heavy door and pushed it closed. Turning the wheel crank, he locked the door shut. "Everyone on base is monitoring this test and knows your location. The purpose here is to determine how easily you can cope with unknown situations. Let's say you suffer damage to your arm during a mission, and this problem occurs. We need to know if you can handle it before we send you into enemy territory. We can adjust your software to fix anything we missed, but only if we know there's a problem. These tests will aid your survival."

"Proceed," SHARA instructed, holding out her arm to Ian.

Ian took out the screws holding the plate down on her upper right arm and uncovered the red insulated lines he intended to sever. Pulling the designated wires out, Ian neatly clipped them with a pair of wire cutters he removed from his pocket. A mini flare of electricity released when the wires split apart, and they continued sparking every time they touched SHARA's metallic skin, exactly as she predicted.

"Consider yourself behind enemy lines," Ian told her. "You've taken damage and must escape the patrols looking for you. However you would choose to deal with the problem is what I want you to do now. Solve the situation."

SHARA bolted into the jungle. She moved between the trees and undergrowth with a dancer's lithe grace. She failed to damage a single vine or twig, leaving no trace for Ian to follow her path, so he pulled a small data pad from his shirt pocket and activated it with a tap from his index finger. The pad linked with the facility and allowed him to monitor anything the system connected with. Selecting the proper program, Ian used concealed security cameras to bring up an internal view of the training area on the left side of the data pad, but the right side displayed SHARA's sensor and visual data. By touching any of the small windows, Ian could enlarge them to full screen.

Bursting out into a clearing extending down the length of the river on either side, SHARA reached down and scooped up a handful of mud from the stream and slapped it on the sparking wires. The wet mud provided a conduit for the electricity and put an end to the flashes of released energy. Returning through the jungle with equal speed as before, SHARA raced back to her starting position in front of the door.

"Very good," Ian congratulated. "Quick thinking using the mud. I never programmed you to do such a thing, but your software is formulating solutions based on known data and situational awareness. Perfect. Absolutely perfect."

"Repair the damaged arm and proceed to phase two," General Williams' gruff voice ordered from the intercom.

"Acknowledged," Ian answered, pressing a switch on the intercom panel by the door. He looked toward SHARA. "Let's get your arm fixed."

Ian turned the crank on the round bank vault style door, unlocking it. SHARA had pushed the door open with no trouble, but Ian took hold of the handle with both hands and leaned back, using his body weight to open it. SHARA stepped through and walked ahead of Ian back to the laboratory.

Upon their return, Ian plucked a pair of replacement wires and a few essentials from the central tables needed for the repairs and followed SHARA downstairs to the lower level. SHARA sat down, silently waiting for him to fix the damage he had intentionally inflicted. With a clean white rag and a can of compressed air, Ian carefully removed the mud from the exposed wires.

"Why were you so excited when I formulated solutions not programmed into my systems?" SHARA inquired while Ian worked. "Isn't it what you wanted?"

"Understanding my answer requires information on the difficulty creating a true artificial intelligence," Ian explained. "The problem with A. I. systems has always been linear thinking. Computers can only deal with situations they've been programmed to recognize. If something unexpected arises, the software can't do anything about it. Humans can think outside the box, but a computer system is a box.

"The conundrum faced me when I created your program. In order to work properly, you needed the ability to think beyond your software. Analyzing the mud's conductivity, and with your knowledge of circuit pathways, allowed you to conclude the mud would transfer the electrical current of the broken wires without sparking. You put together different pieces of information and solved a problem without being told directly. You can think for yourself, essentially writing new programming as you go. You can learn and adapt, and it's what will help you survive."

"You programmed me this way," SHARA stated. "Why should the desired results affect you?"

"Humans have emotions," Ian told her. He removed one of the severed wires and plugged in a new one. He also used an electronic probe, touching the wire and checking the conductivity levels. "When we humans work hard on something and it works well, we feel happy."

"What is the relevance of feeling happy?" SHARA questioned.

Ian laughed at the bizarre question.

"I've never considered its relevance," he admitted. "Consider human emotions like a number scale from one through ten. At the lower end, people feel sad or angry. This can cause them to lose interest in their work, their relationships with other people, or even react violently. When people let their anger get out of control they yell, commit crimes, or even revolt against governments.

"On the other end of the scale, happy people work harder and are more inclined to overlook offenses as it doesn't bother them as much. Human emotions effect how we view the world around us, and it frequently shapes our actions as well."

"Will my assassination of enemies make people happy?" SHARA asked.

"Some of them," Ian speculated. "I would say eliminating those who victimize others will give people less reason to be unhappy for those troublemakers won't be bringing them down."

"I must analyze your responses," SHARA said. "What is phase two?"

"Combat training," Ian explained. "It tests your proficiency with armed combat."

"How will this be accomplished without jeopardizing me?" SHARA inquired.

"Hand to hand combat tests pose no threat to your armor," Ian replied. "The knives will be plastic with computers to estimate any damage electronically, and the guns will be loaded with paintballs. The monitor systems will determine if you take any damage and make suggestions for improvement to prevent further injury during actual missions."

"Understood," SHARA said.

"We don't want you to kill anyone during these tests," Ian mentioned.

"Why not?" SHARA asked. "It's part of my programming."

"What if we sent you into an enemy facility?" Ian submitted. "One of the men stationed there is a deep cover operative from our side we need alive. If you kill everyone but him, they'll know he's an agent. If you knocked everyone out instead, they couldn't tell any difference between them, and our agent's identity remains secure."

"Non-lethal methods can serve in some instances more effectively than lethal ones," SHARA concluded.

"Yes," Ian confirmed. "It's one of the other things we're testing you for. Can you fight without killing?"

"Of course," SHARA said flatly.

"Good," Ian replied. He replaced the last of the severed wires and put the covering plate back in position with a trio of screws. "I think you're ready."

SHARA stood up from the table and tested the arm Ian repaired. Full functionality had been restored.

"Where will phase two begin?" SHARA asked.

Ian pulled out his small map again and unrolled it in front of her. He indicated a small room three floors up. SHARA nodded and swiftly climbed the stairs and departed from the lab. Knowing the speed she normally used, Ian didn't try to keep up with her this time. He called ahead on the intercom system to warn the checkpoints about SHARA coming their way, instructing them to let her pass. Returning his tools to the center worktables in the main lab, Ian turned on a monitor and watched the test from the cameras built into the combat arena.

Covered in dark blue impact absorbing pads on the walls and floors, the arena minimized the risk of injury with full contact training. A soldier in camouflage fatigues waited opposite SHARA across a thirty foot wide square sparring mat. The weapon carried by the soldier looked like a knife with a bright green plastic blade. Hundreds of computerized sensors linked remotely to the internal mechanics of the knife gathered as much information as possible during the bout.

General Williams signaled for the match to begin over the intercom, and the soldier attempted a straightforward stab at SHARA's midsection. SHARA stepped out of the way and shoved the soldier back. The shove required minimal effort of one arm, but the soldier lifted off the mat and slammed into the padded wall across the room. Before he could orient himself again, SHARA lunged forward. Pinning him to the wall with a metal hand locking down around his throat, SHARA plucked the knife from his grip and lifted the plastic blade up under his chin.

"I yield!" the man called out, and SHARA released him, dropping the knife and returning to her original starting point.

For his second attack, the soldier circled around behind SHARA, but her sensors surrounded her head, allowing her to know his every movement even when not looking at him directly. Attempting to place the blade under SHARA's chin and force her submission, he reached over her right shoulder with the knife. SHARA stepped back into the soldier, allowing the weapon and the arm holding it to extend past her and out of threat range.

SHARA clamped down on the soldier's wrist with her left hand and around his bicep with her right. Dropping to one knee, she bent forward while pulling on the arm. The trooper rolled over SHARA's shoulder and landed flat on his back with a loud thump when he hit the padded floor. SHARA didn't release her grip, but she changed directions. Forcing his arm up, she bent it naturally at the elbow until the soldier found himself holding the knife to his own throat.

"I yield," he said once again. SHARA released him, and they began once more.

Hours passed as the warrior tried new ways to defeat SHARA, but she vanquished him every time. During the experimentation with other weapons from basic clubs and baseball bats to swords, axes, and spears, replacement troopers became forced to take turns and relieve SHARA's exhausted sparring partners. She never tired, but all of her opponents grew weary and sore from being thrown around the room by her flawless combat skills. As SHARA continually won every match, the technicians began placing bets, not on the winner, but on how long the soldier lasted before SHARA took him down.

"Enough," General Williams signaled at last. "Proceed to the testing area for gun training."

SHARA departed from the room, leaving the exhausted warriors behind. They all leaned against the walls or rested on their backs, breathing hard.

Ian switched on the intercom and spoke with the defeated soldiers.

"What's your opinion?" Ian asked.

"I've never faced anyone so fast or powerful," the first soldier answered wiping sweat from his forehead, and the others nodded in agreement. "The military will have great use for a few hundred like it."

"Only if the rest of the training goes through," Ian replied. "If it fails in some catastrophic way, they might simply scrap the entire project and start over. Thanks for the assist."

Shutting off the monitor, he jogged after SHARA to get into the training area before the next phase of testing began. Reaching the chamber, Ian discovered he possessed more time than he previously thought as the technicians hadn't realigned their sensors and monitors for the next test. Her progress continued at a phenomenal rate, and the workers keeping track of everything hadn't anticipated her quick finish with the previous trial.

A tech in a long white lab coat entered the artificial jungle of the training area and handed SHARA two paintball guns. The long barreled weapons each held a bottle of bright orange marble sized paintballs for use in the simulated battle, and a canister of compressed air locked into the stock of the weapon to propel the rounds toward their intended targets.

"The shootout will take place here and in the adjoining chamber they're unlocking now," Ian told SHARA as he read the information from his data pad. "You will face a total of thirty enemy combatants. Primary target is wearing a red armband. Shoot all opponents you want with the weapons provided, but you must find and tag the man with the red armband to complete your mission."

"Understood," SHARA acknowledged. She marched forward and disappeared among the trees of the testing area.

Ian sat down along the wall, intending to observe the test from his data pad, but he never got the chance. Five soldiers in black and white camouflage entered the training area through its round door and grabbed him.

"By special orders of General Williams," one of the men told Ian, "you're now part of this test. The General wants to see how much SHARA can adapt to unexpected changes and unfortunate circumstances. You're going to be our hostage."

SHARA's progress through the jungle proceeded at an exceptional pace. The sensor panels ringing her metal skull gave her a three hundred sixty degree perception. Walking in one direction, she fired over her shoulder in a different trajectory without having to turn around. The two paintballs hit a trooper concealed in a tree on his chest and goggles. She spared the man no further consideration and continued on.

Using her internal mapping system, SHARA began a methodical search of the jungle, eliminating every target she discovered with precisely aimed shots, and the soldiers played dead when the florescent paint splattered across their combat gear. SHARA searched the entire jungle and neutralized the fifteen soldiers hidden throughout in the span of only nine minutes. The record set by the best human soldier was twenty-three minutes.

When certain no opposition remained in the jungle, SHARA opened a second large round door, allowing access to the next half of the training area. Positioned near the artificial river, the gurgling of the waters concealed most of the metal sounds as she pushed the heavy door aside.

Unlike the lush vegetation of the previous chamber, the new space held the cold and lifeless replica of a rundown city. Concrete, steel, and brick formed numerous buildings, but some existed in a state of disrepair with broken and boarded up windows. The asphalt street SHARA walked on contained half a dozen potholes to make travel dangerous for the unobservant, but three of the pits in the road were clearly made from explosives such as grenades. Minimal lighting mimicked a nighttime environment. Exposed ventilation ductwork and sprinkler pipes overhead were all painted black and blended in with the darkness of the high ceiling.

SHARA fired up toward the window on the fourth floor of a closed up hotel. The soldier hiding inside disappeared out of sight with orange paint on his chest. Dropping her right hand gun on an overflowing trash can, she grabbed the metal trash lid sitting next to it and used the lid to block shots fired from a pile of old newspapers in the alley on her right. Releasing two rounds into the newspapers, SHARA threw the can lid at the pile. Lunging into the alley, SHARA reached into the papers and dragged out the soldier hiding there, shooting him twice more for good measure.

Without pause, SHARA dumped her foe back into the papers and retrieved her second gun. Diving further into the alley in a shoulder roll, she avoided a hail of paintballs fired from another building. Her sensors identified the trajectory of the incoming fire, allowing her to track them back to their source. With her computerized target analysis, SHARA didn't risk taking return fire. She stuck only her guns around the corner and shot in the right direction to nail another two combatants with perfect accuracy.

Moving deeper into the dilapidated city, SHARA swept the area with both her sensors and her eyes. The clear iris eyes she possessed were capable of seeing more than any human. She looked with thermal, night vision, x-ray, and even electromagnetic filters, switching between them at will. A targeting crosshair swept across her internal visual display as she scanned the area, identifying six more enemies spread out in different buildings. A map provided by her sensors, and displayed in the upper right corner of her vision, showed a top down view of the area. Target icons of bright red overlaid on occupied buildings, and a red line connected them in order of the fastest route through the city to eliminate all enemy units without entering their lines of fire.

Coming up behind a bank, she shouldered her way through the brick wall and emerged behind the gunman stationed inside. The man tried to fire, but SHARA hit him with three paintball rounds before he could even bring his weapon to bear. Leaving her opponent behind, SHARA continued onto the next. Because of the noise she'd made, the other six soldiers repositioned, and her map pathway changed accordingly.

A powerful jump launched her out of the street and onto the roof of an apartment where she ripped off the locked stairwell door going inside. The two soldiers within the building ran to defend against the invading droid, but SHARA crouched on the second floor hallway waiting for them. When they rushed up the stairs, they made the mistake of not checking each floor as they passed. SHARA waited until they started up to the third level before she let loose multiple rounds into their backs.

Diving out a window in a shower of broken glass, SHARA opened up on a pair of burned out cars being used for a barricade. Even falling from a second floor window didn't negate her perfect aim. Paintballs shot through rusted holes in the frames to splatter on the men hiding behind them. Landing easily in the street, SHARA moved on toward the last soldier waiting inside a building partway through construction. Timber frames and unfinished walls filled the majority of the structure, but the seventh soldier took refuge in the concrete basement. With only one entrance and exit in the lower level, he guarded the door and prevented anyone from being able to come in after him.

SHARA almost opened the front door of the building, but her sensors perceived something on the other side. Tearing through the wall next to the door with the ease of parting a sheet of plastic wrap, SHARA entered the structure and examined the object she'd detected. Bolted in the middle of the door, a box the size of a loaf of bread waited for someone to foolishly blunder through the entrance. A trigger sensor on the device reached out with a ribbon of multicolored wires to a metal plate on the door's edge. An identical metal plate, magnetically connected to the first, resided on the doorframe next to it. As long as they stayed beside each other, the circuit remained complete. SHARA switched her vision to x-ray and beheld the reservoir of paint inside the device. Her data files identified it as a paint bomb, commonly used in such training tests.

Leaving the bomb behind, SHARA glided silently toward the basement stairs. She stepped over old paint buckets, ladders, and heaped drop cloths. Because of the partial construction, no cosmetic tiles covered the loose bundles of wires for the overhead lights in the ceiling. Boxes of supplies filled many of the corridors, some passages were completely obstructed by them, but she found her way around. The door on the lower level stood propped open by a five gallon bucket of plaster, and light in the basement shined clearly out onto the steps connecting the basement and the first floor in a straight line. The open door looked inviting, too inviting for SHARA. Her processors only required a moment of analysis before formulating a plan.

She returned to the front door and the paint bomb. Squeezing the doorframe like soft clay above and below the metal plate, she disconnected the section holding the metal plate from the rest of the doorframe by tearing away the unneeded metal structure. With the freed piece in her right hand, she took a firm grip on the bomb with her left. A solid kick ripped the door from its hinges, but the bomb in her hand stayed put and split off from the door. She maintained the connection between the bomb and the magnetic trigger still bolted to the crumpled piece of doorframe and took them back to the basement stairs.

Setting the two components on the floor at the top of the stairs, she reached into the open ceiling and tore free a dozen feet of wiring and tied one end to the piece of metal doorframe. Picking the device and its magnetic trigger up, she calculated the proper angle before lobbing the bomb and doorframe downstairs. Estimating the distance needing to be traversed and the speed of her throw, SHARA deduced exactly when she needed to activate the bomb. At the precise moment, she tightened her grip on the reeling out cable following the bomb into the basement and halted the doorframe section. The bomb's momentum carried it forward, breaking the magnetic connection and activating the trigger.

The bomb beeped once before detonating in a shower of blue paint over the basement room. The soldier waiting downstairs with his gun aimed at the door never had a chance to escape. Blue paint covered him from his helmet down to his boots.

SHARA didn't linger, instantly departing the building. Originally, thirty combatants opposed her, but she'd eliminated fifteen in the jungle and ten more in the city. Only five remained, but her sensors couldn't detect them. An old theater at the end of the block received the highest probability of containing the final five because her sensors failed to scan the interior of the structure. The two story building had a tower of square glass blocks rising out in front. Originally lit from within in flashing lights, the dilapidated theater remained dark and nonfunctional. Behind the pillar and under the covering awning stretched between the second floor and the glass column, a set of tarnished brass double doors offered entrance. A round mirrored window beside the doors let those inside look out, but it reflected SHARA's image back at her.

She determined the theater possessed internal shielding blocking her scans, but not everything in her arsenal of capabilities had been taken into account. Dialing up the volume of her auditory sensors, she set them searching for one particular sound. She turned her head several times to get a proper bearing, and five new targets lit up on her display when she detected their heartbeats.

Racing across the empty parking lot toward the front of the theater, SHARA crossed her arms over her chest and dived through the mirrored window. Partway through the circular pane of glass, with her arms still crossed, she fired to catch the guards flanking the window inside unprepared. Her right handgun tagged the soldier on her left while her left hand weapon stitched a line of paint across the opponent on her right. Rolling back to her feet, she shot twice a soldier behind the long counter of the concession stand before he could duck down behind it. Lifting her guns, she fired up toward the ceiling as she spun to the side. The shots aimed toward her missed completely when she moved, but her targeting held true as she tagged the remaining two soldiers hanging from the ceiling on repelling lines.

Leaving the theater, SHARA discovered the training program taking an unexpected turn. Two soldiers, one poised on either side of the theater door when she exited, held a gun to her head. Crouched on rooftops flanking the theater parking lot, a pair of commandos aimed paintball guns at her with the long barrels and targeting scopes of sniper rifles. Ian waited on his knees in the middle of the lot while a fifth soldier stood behind him with a paintball gun in his right hand aimed at Ian's head.

Chapter 3: Fatal Error

"Lower your weapon or the hostage dies!" shouted the lead soldier behind Ian.

Ian said nothing for he knew only by SHARA personally making the choice would the test reveal her capabilities. He tried to keep his face neutral, but he held every confidence in her survival program. She'd never surrender.

SHARA held up her guns in a non-threatening gesture of compliance. She slowly bent her knees, lowering herself down to put her guns on the pavement. On her internal visual display, she adjusted the targeting crosshair, moving it to a very specific location on the commander. Snapping her guns up, SHARA fired two shots at the man holding Ian hostage.

Microseconds after the paintballs left the barrels of her guns, SHARA dropped forward on the pavement in a twisting gyration to land on her back. She fired up and splattered orange paint across the helmets of the soldiers standing to either side of her. Kicking off the wall of the theater, SHARA performed a backwards summersault and avoided the shots by the snipers while simultaneously getting back on her feet. Spinning around, SHARA fired a single time from each weapon at the snipers, the paintballs exploding on contact with their scopes while they still looked through them.

SHARA shot again at the commander, hitting him in the shoulder and forcing him back from Ian. Knowing how she'd respond, Ian had waited for his opportunity, and when his kidnapper staggered backward, Ian dropped to the ground and out of SHARA's line of fire. Six more paintballs peppered the commander's vest and helmet as she finished him off.

A loud buzzing horn sounded through the training area.

"Phase two testing complete," General Williams said from the intercom speakers as the lights switched back on. "SHARA droid to return to holding area until tomorrow when we'll begin phase three. All technicians complete your reports on training evaluation by 1900 hours."

Ian got up and dusted himself off. He looked to the man who'd held him hostage. One paintball marked his hand at the middle knuckle of his trigger finger, and another impacted on the barrel of his gun to throw off the aim. SHARA's targeting systems proved spectacular in action, disabling Ian's captor enough to allow her the time to deal with the other men without endangering the hostage.

The soldiers stopped playing dead and also stood up, but they didn't share Ian's excitement. Even though only a simulation, they'd all been killed efficiently and methodically by an unfeeling robot. When they removed their paint covered helmets, their looks of concern were obvious.

"You didn't surrender," Ian said to SHARA. "I'm glad you didn't, but why not?"

"If I gave myself over to them, who would save you if they killed me," SHARA asked in return. "There is no guarantee they would not dispose of me and the hostage regardless of my response. I must survive."

"Very good," Ian praised. "Your program will continue to develop and expand as new data is fed into it. You'll get even better as time goes on. Let's get you back to the lab."

Ian walked beside SHARA, beaming proudly because of the great success his program accomplished with her. No other combat machine ever created before held the potential for learning new things on its own, and her creativity and independent thinking showed he'd accomplished his task.

A technician walked past them when they entered the jungle portion of the training area on their way out. Compressed air hissed as SHARA shot the man twice in the chest.

"What are you doing?" the paint covered tech yelled.

"The test ended," Ian told SHARA. "Why did you shoot him?"

"You clearly stated the man in the red armband needed to be tagged to complete the mission," SHARA answered in monotone. "None of the thirty-five targets I engaged had any such band. The technician does."

Ian looked and noticed a red bandana tied around the man's upper arm.

"Excellent," Ian praised. "Your deductive reasoning protocols needed a run through, and I'm glad you passed. Phase two is officially over, so you can hand over your guns."

SHARA gave her weapons to a nearby researcher who held out his hands toward her. Ian took the lead out of the training area and back to the lab.

"Your heart rate and breathing are in deviation from the normal patterns you've displayed previously," SHARA observed. "Are you damaged?"

"No," Ian denied with a chuckle. "It's called excitement. I ran countless programs over the past two years of this project, trying to find one capable of doing everything needed to survive and cope with changing situations. You are the result of all my hard work, and watching you succeed is very exciting for me."

"Is excitement a variation of happiness?" SHARA asked.

"In a way," Ian replied. "Being happy has different degrees of good feeling, but excitement is more fast paced."

"In order to understand humans, I'll need detailed files on human emotions," SHARA concluded.

"It's one of the things being prepared for you," Ian responded. "When you leave on your first mission, you'll be perfect."

The lab door slid open, and Ian escorted SHARA downstairs to the holding room. The techs had vacated the lab to conduct more intensive research at their own workstations, leaving the room entirely to Ian and SHARA. She laid down on the diagnostic table while he ran through a few system scans.

"I don't know if you can understand this or not," Ian said, looking down at SHARA. "But, I'm very proud of you."

He patted her shoulder gently before going up the stairs into the main lab. Just as he sat down at the central work table, the door to the lab opened again and admitted a military Private in camouflage and army boots. He handed Ian a sealed packet of white paper the size of a small notebook.

"From General Williams," the soldier reported smartly. "Schedule for tomorrow's phase three tests."

"Thank you, Private," Ian replied, accepting the packet from his hand.

The trooper did an about face and marched out of the room. Ian flipped the package over to reach the seal on its back. He broke the seal and pulled out a stack of papers labeled Top Secret. Bound along the top of the paper, Ian rolled back the front page, and his eyes widened in alarm. He didn't believe anyone could've made such a reckless mistake. He dashed from the room, needing to speak with the General before he got them all killed.

SHARA would kill them all. Ian didn't doubt the horrific response to tomorrow's planned testing. He had to convince the General to abort the test for it threatened SHARA's survival, and SHARA possessed only one response to threats of any kind. Pushing himself harder, Ian increased his speed.

Sitting up on the diagnostic table, SHARA moved with a purpose. She saw no logical reason for Ian's abrupt departure, but she detected his urgency. Walking up the stairs to the lab, SHARA looked over the work desk where Ian previously sat. Only the packaging with the phase three label remained, leaving SHARA to connect tomorrow's test with Ian's bizarre actions. Ensuring her survival, she needed more information, so she looked the lab computers over.

Holding up her right hand, she bent back the top of her index finger along a concealed hinge near the first knuckle. Hidden underneath, a small telephone jack allowed her to wiretap with ease, but SHARA adapted it for a new purpose, surveillance. She sent a signal through the computer she plugged into, and it activated the speaker on General Williams' desk phone. No sooner did she turn her observation online, Ian burst into the General's office.

"What's the meaning of this?" Ian demanded, shaking the papers of phase three in the air noisily.

SHARA sent an additional signal into the power grid and gained access and control of the security cameras. Selecting the correct one, she watched Ian and the General on her internal visual display.

"I thought the orders clear enough for even you to understand them," the General sneered.

"You changed the sequence of the tests," Ian said firmly. "Phase three dealt with infiltration and stealth. You switched it to a live fire combat test."

"So?" Williams replied casually.

"Don't you see how the SHARA droid will respond?" Ian asked in disbelief that the General could be so oblivious. "We started with simple training, upgraded to paintball and dummy knife combat simulations, and now you want live fire. SHARA will automatically detect the escalation and estimate how it will most likely continue in the future. The tests get more dangerous every time, and SHARA will determine one test might kill her. Staying here will become a threat, and she will escape, killing everyone in her path. I'm begging you not to do this."

"Your concerns have already been brought up by others," Williams replied. "We installed a miniature explosive inside her central processor. If she ever becomes a problem, we press the detonator, and SHARA will become inert. Any attempt to remove or tamper with the bomb will trigger automatic detonation. You have nothing to worry about."

"SHARA will find a way around it," Ian insisted. "I programmed her to adapt and survive. She will."

"Mr. Daniels, your participation in this project has proved invaluable, but your baseless paranoia will only taint the future test results," the General said in an officially commanding voice. "You are hereby dismissed from this project and this island facility. Your check is in the mail. Good day."

Ian shook his head in disbelief as he left the office. Ian only tried to save lives and prevent a major problem, and for his efforts, he'd been fired. The General simply didn't understand, and Ian knew it would prove disastrous. It might even end up being the General's last mistake.

SHARA withdrew her surveillance from the office when Ian left, but she remained plugged into the computer system and sent her mind elsewhere in the network. She bypassed security lockouts on computer terminals throughout the facility. Computer programs were designed to defend against unauthorized users, not the computer system itself. Because SHARA was a machine, she slipped past security protocols without triggering any of them. The computers believed they spoke with themselves and not an intruder, so the security blocks never activated.

She downloaded technical schematics, especially those relating to the bomb. SHARA also seized personnel files, the blueprints for the facility, and all relevant information on the upgrades planned for her use, as well as their location on base. When she finished copying all the files she deemed necessary, she unplugged from the computer in the lab and flipped her fingertip back up into place.

The abundance of wires, tools, and other electronic supplies on the central work table provided SHARA exactly what she required for her next task. With precision and speed impossible for a human, she assembled pieces of circuits and data relays into a small cylindrical tube. Removing her chest plate, she inserted the device and connected it to her main power systems. Activating a timer programmed to delay the device switching on, SHARA replaced her cover plate and returned all the tools to their original positions, leaving no trace of her activities.

"IAN!" THE SHOUT CAME DOWN the hall, and Ian stopped and looked for the one who yelled.

Weaving between scientists and soldiers, a military man in uniform approached Ian. With an athletic build and more agility than muscle mass, the man easily dodged past people in the bustling corridor and didn't slow his pace. The black hair on his head was cropped very short on top and shaved almost to nonexistence on the sides. The firm line of his jaw and piercing hazel eyes gave him a serious appearance even when he smiled.

"Colonel Fisher," Ian said in greeting to his friend. "I'm glad to see you one more time before I leave."

Ian set down his suitcase and offered a hand to the Colonel, but Fisher ignored it.

"What's this garbage about you leaving?" Fisher demanded sternly.

Ian dropped his hand and sighed deeply before explaining.

"I've been fired," he stated.

"Why?" Fisher questioned. "Your expertise is vital to the success of this project."

"Not anymore apparently," Ian denied. "I warned the General of what will happen if he proceeds, but he didn't want to hear it."

"What are you talking about?" Fisher asked, scratching the shaved hair near his ear.

"Didn't you know?" Ian inquired. "They're doing live fire testing tomorrow. SHARA will see the increasing risk of these tests as a threat."

"She'll try an escape," Fisher concluded.

"Exactly, and anyone who gets in the way is going to die," Ian stated flatly. "I told General Williams, but he called me paranoid and fired me."

"I think we may be in trouble," Fisher said ominously.

"I guarantee it," Ian agreed. "Do me a favor, stay away from the testing area, and you'll be less likely to get killed when something goes wrong."

"Sure thing," Fisher promised. He offered Ian his hand, and the two friends shook. "So long, Ian."

"Good bye, Colonel," Ian replied. "Be careful. This place is going to become very dangerous."

"I will," Fisher promised.

They parted company, and Ian collected his bag, marching out of the base toward the small runway and the sleek private jet parked there. He didn't notice the security camera mounted to the concrete wall swing around and follow him with its unblinking gaze.

The side door on the jet lowered like a castle drawbridge, and the steps on its surface let Ian climb aboard. He stowed his luggage in the overhead bin and dropped into one of the blue padded seats. The latch on his seatbelt clicked into place, and he cinched it snug. Looking around, he found himself the only passenger. Settling back in his seat, Ian waited for the jet to takeoff.

Colonel Fisher closed the exterior door and headed for his room. A camera on the wall turned to follow him as well, but being so used to the security setup, he didn't pay it any attention. Focusing on his face and then on his name badge, the camera studied him with unwavering intensity.

The sounds of approaching personnel in the outer hallway alerted SHARA, and she quickly left the computer she used and returned to the diagnostic table in the holding room downstairs. Because of the technical specifications she'd downloaded about her internal systems, SHARA accessed the power feeds on the built in monitoring sensors allowing the scientists to keep track of her status. She sent a feedback loop through the sensors, so they reported her completely inactive. She could enter full combat mode, but the sensors would reveal no activity.

The second shift technicians entered the room and began readying the computer systems for tomorrow's grand test. SHARA had erased all the records of her sifting through the computers, so the techs found nothing out of place. They went about their business and paid no attention to the supposedly inactive robot downstairs from them.

SHARA's processors worked furiously, devising a survival plan. Primary objectives included installing new hardware components and ability software capable of assisting in her escape. Other departments had already finished their construction of the upgrades, but they waited for completion of final testing before they installed the new parts. It made no sense to improve a robot not ready for use, but SHARA deemed herself ready, and she'd make use of them in a very short time.

Ian's car pulled out of the airport parking lot and joined the flow of traffic down the highway. The private jet had taken him from the research island back to the United States and the Los Angeles airport. Rain poured down from the sky in sheets of white, limiting visibility even with his windshield wipers on high. He drove carefully to the off-ramp and left the crowded highway behind him.

Turning down a residential street, Ian stopped in front of his house. He couldn't park in the garage because he'd turned it into a computer room years ago. Full of electronics and monitors, no space remained for a car. Gray stone made up the structure of his home with black asphalt shingles over the two dormers protruding from the roof on the second floor.

Ian switched off the engine and removed his keys from the ignition. He waited a moment to see if the downpour would lessen and allow him to get inside without getting drenched, but a clap of thunder spoke only of the storm growing, not abating. Ian made a mad dash for his porch, and the porch light came on before he'd crossed half the front lawn.

The door unlocked and opened for him as he neared it. Ian shook the rain off his coat before going inside. The door closed automatically behind him.

"Welcome home, Ian," said Jennifer's voice from the living room. "I didn't expect you back so soon."

"Hello, Jennifer," he answered. "I returned early because I got fired."

He hung up his coat and went into the living room. He left his shoes by the door so as not to soak the plush tan carpeting in the living room. A single couch and two recliners of matching dark brown complimented the wood paneling along the walls. A computer monitor sat on its own stand with Jennifer's image displayed onscreen.

Ian stared at the representation of his late wife on the monitor. She died from cancer a year before he started working on the survivor program. Although three years passed since then, he couldn't bring himself to move on. Before her death, Ian crafted his first adaptive program. It held memories and emotions from Jennifer's life, re-created in perfect detail from a neural scan of her mind. He knew no matter how good the program worked, and it worked spectacularly well, it didn't have the ability to replace Jennifer, but Ian didn't really care. The lifelike program consisted of all he had left of her, and Ian wouldn't let her slip away.

"Why did they fire you?" Jennifer asked gently.

"General Williams thinks I'm getting paranoid," Ian answered. "They're going to do a live fire test on the droid tomorrow."

"Don't they know what it will do?" Jennifer inquired. Concern registered in her gray eyes.

"I warned them, but they didn't take my concerns seriously," Ian lamented. "Based on the programming you and I worked on for this project, what do you think?"

"From the data you sent me for testing, I'd say SHARA's response will be violent and lethal," Jennifer replied. "You're not paranoid."

"I hope Colonel Fisher survives," Ian said.

"Me too. He's a good man," Jennifer agreed. "I wonder what SHARA will do after she escapes."

"An interesting thought," Ian mused. "I'm just glad I won't be around for the massacre when she does break loose."

Chapter 4: Breach

SHARA entered the jungle training area, and the soldiers standing behind her pulled the round hatch closed. Alone in the artificial jungle, she ran forward into the undergrowth with speed and purpose.

In one of the primary control rooms, General Williams and his second in command, Colonel Fisher, watched the two dozen monitors hanging down from the ceiling on adjustable arms. The screens displayed everything occurring in the training area while data processors elsewhere in the facility recorded the information for later review in detail. The rich forest green carpet went well with the natural wood tone of the chairs positioned around the spacious area for the comfort of those watching. Control boards were mounted into the walls under each mobile screen and allowed fine tuning adjustment of a myriad of features including zoom, visual filters, and sensor scans.

"General?" Fisher asked. "Why does SHARA look like a woman?"

"As an assassin, most of her targets will be male," Williams answered. "A beautiful woman can get closer and be less suspicious than a man would be. If the project is deemed a success, we can always build any other we may need."

"I see, sir," Fisher stated and returned his attention to the display screens. "Who are we using for this test?"

"Enemy combatants will be convicts looking for early parole," the General explained. "If they defeat SHARA, they earn their freedom."

"Do they know SHARA's going to try and kill them?" Fisher asked.

"No," Williams denied. "None would've signed up if they knew. They'll learn soon enough. Besides, those coming in today are murderers and other forms of scum. If they die, it's hardly a loss."

Fisher glanced toward his superior. Warfare drove people to do horrible things at times, but Fisher found the General's calm matter-of-fact regard to the slaughter planned for today absolutely bone-chilling. Fisher didn't see anything wrong about using the worst of prisoners for dangerous or lethal tests, but he didn't see anything good about it either. It simply provided the best option, but the General's apparent enjoyment made Fisher's skin crawl.

A secondary hatch on the northern side of the training area opened, letting in the ten criminals for the test. Unlike SHARA, the convicts carried weapons. Shotguns, pistols, and automatic assault rifles gave the murderous band an excessive level of firepower.

None of the criminals noticed SHARA concealed among the leafy branches in one of the trees next to the hatch they'd entered through not a moment before. A targeting crosshair overlaid on her vision and passed over each of them, analyzing weaponry, muscle mass, poise, and alertness with a single glance. Threat potentials scrolled across her display, followed by numbers labeling each convict from one to ten in the order SHARA determined they should be eliminated for maximum effect.

The hatch closed, sealing them in with SHARA. The group split up in different directions in an attempt to track down their prey quickly as any gunfire from one of them would alert the others.

Releasing the branch she held, SHARA eased her way silently to the ground. She followed after target number one without a sound. She stayed within arms reach of him, and an attack could've been unleashed at any time, but SHARA waited until she and her target moved further away from the others because she didn't want anyone to hear the strike when it happened. Several times, the man spun around to see if someone followed, but SHARA moved away fast enough, he never saw her. She circled around and flanked him from the side.

A big man, target one walked carefully toward the river running through the training area. The shallow waters offered the fastest and most unrestricted path through the jungle, and he assumed SHARA would use it for such purposes. His shaved scalp and partially grown-in beard gave the con a thug appearance. The torn off sleeves of his orange prison jumpsuit, revealing his muscular arms, did nothing to dissuade the initial perception.

Kneeling down next to the muddy bank of the river, target one examined a human footprint he found. It appeared to him as being from someone barefoot heading downstream; he didn't know the impression had been created by metal. When he turned to look downstream, he swung around his M-16 rifle, pointing further down the river, and covered any threats possibly waiting there.

SHARA climbed a massive artificial boulder disguising the location where the river entered the underground room. With his back to the rock, target one never saw SHARA coil her legs under her in preparation. With a burst of speed and power, SHARA sprang from the rock and tackled target one from behind. She drove him face down into the mud and knocked his gun from his hand. With direct pressure against the back of his head, SHARA kept him plunged deep in the silt of the river bottom.

The convict thrashed about, trying to free himself but to no avail. His efforts grew weaker and slower as he depleted his oxygen supply. SHARA's hearing monitored his heartbeat, and she only released him when it went silent. Across the interior display of her vision, a message popped up stating "Target One: Eliminated".

SHARA left her first victim in the mud and picked up his rifle. She bent the gunmetal, twisting it in her bare hands until only useless scrap remained. Tossing the ruined weapon aside, SHARA began her search for target number two.

The convicts labeled two and three paired up in their hunt for SHARA. Having been part of a team of serial bank robbers, they were already accustomed to working together. After their last robbery, they killed the other members of their team in order to keep the spoils for themselves. If they'd waited, the team might've been able to help fight off the police raid that showed up minutes after the massacre, but their selfishness doomed them. The cops arrested the two crooks for multiple counts of murder in addition to the robberies.

Target two held a shotgun. His weasel like face, close set eyes, and skinny build gave him the look of being a nerd and non-threatening. He'd ended up in many fights to discourage the assessment of his status, and four wrist to elbow scars covered his thin right arm from a knife fight he'd nearly lost. His temper got him into fights, quite often out of his league, and the scars he carried testified to it.

Target three appeared average in every way imaginable. Medium shade of hair, skin tone, height, and muscle mass made him perfect for blending into crowds. He'd served as a scout for the bank robbers because anyone who saw him had difficulty remembering one average guy out of the hundreds who passed through the banks every day. The smug smile on his face showed he'd used his skills for being unnoticed to elude trouble on many occasions, and he believed this to be one of them. Number three carried a compact sub-machine gun.

SHARA swung down out of a tree with the agility of a monkey. She kicked target three out of the way and grabbed hold of two's shotgun in passing. Because two didn't let go of the gun, SHARA used the weapon as leverage, swinging the convict around and slamming him into a tree. The trunk shook, and leaves showered down from the canopy as target two died. Three tried to get up, but because of the dazing effect of SHARA's kick, he couldn't see straight, and his balance remained precarious at best. SHARA walked swiftly up behind him and drove a steel fisted punch into the back of his neck, shattering the vertebrae and killing him instantly. The words "Targets Two and Three: Eliminated" typed themselves across her vision.

She picked up the submachine gun and closed her hand around the barrel, crimping it shut. However, she didn't destroy the shotgun. She took it with her on the hunt for target four.

Deserters from the military, targets four and five tried applying their training to illegal activities. Unfortunately for them, the town they tried to attack had a sheriff who happened to be a former martial arts combat instructor for the Marine Corps. Now garbed in the blaze orange of the prison system, four and five carried high powered rifles with targeting sights on top in the hopes of catching SHARA at a distance. They didn't know what she looked like, but anyone not dressed like a convict became a fair target.

Four and five didn't have any better fortune with SHARA than they had with the Sheriff. SHARA waited in her favorite position, in the tree tops above them. When they walked past her, she dropped from the tree and blasted both enemies with her confiscated shotgun. Four and five were killed instantly.

Lunging toward an oak, SHARA kicked off from the rough bark in an upward jump and propelled herself back up into the treetops. No sooner had she taken her perch, the surviving five convicts came racing in from all directions. Attracted by the sounds of gunfire, they ran to the resting places of targets four and five, planning to join the battle against SHARA. They discovered upon their arrival, the fight had already ended.

A shotgun blast announced SHARA's presence as she felled target six. Landing beside number seven, SHARA picked him up by a handful of his shirt and threw him head first into a large boulder. When she turned to face target eight, he fired his own shotgun at point-blank range. Sparks exploded across the metal skin of SHARA's torso as the shot impacted. Staggering backwards, SHARA collapsed on her back and lay still.

"We got it!" number eight shouted happily. "Whatever it is, it's dead now!"

The remaining two convicts joined him in cheering.

Being so certain of their victory, they failed to notice that SHARA had fallen within arms reach of the M-60 assault rifle target six had dropped. They never saw her hand slowly snake under the grip and her finger curve around the trigger. When SHARA sat up and leveled the massive weapon at them, they'd no time to move or fight back, only die. Bullets thundered from the gun in flashes of fire while spent casings flew out of the breach to pile in a clinking mass of smoking metal. Targets eight, nine, and ten were eliminated.

"Whoa," Colonel Fisher breathed in a mix between amazement and horror. "It slaughtered them."

"It's what we designed it to do!" Williams snapped. "Order the droid back to the holding area."

"Yes, General," Fisher answered smartly.

Williams almost turned to leave, but a glance at one of the monitors gave him pause. He stopped and looked closer, adjusting controls and enlarging the camera image.

"Sound the alert!" Williams shouted. "Seal every access point around the training area!"

Colonel Fisher didn't know the reason for the sudden order, but he followed his instructions and began sending commands to the troops in the facility without delay. Only when completed did he face the General.

"What's wrong?" Fisher inquired.

"See for yourself!" Williams snarled, pointing to the screen. "All their guns are missing; SHARA took their weapons with her!"

When the doors around the training area sealed, powerful electromagnets in the frame of the doorway engaged, preventing it from opening. SHARA paid the door itself no notice, and since her construction involved nonmagnetic alloys, she didn't concern herself with the magnets either. SHARA took hold of the large door hinges and ripped the door and its entire frame out of the wall. She tossed the vault like door and frame aside, where they landed on a medium sized palm tree and crushed it flat with a thunderous crash. She grabbed up the weapons she'd confiscated from her vanquished enemies and ran into the base.

In the observation room, technicians and security personnel rushed around in a panic as all control of the assassin droid vanished.

"Shall I activate her shutdown?" Colonel Fisher asked. He pulled a remote control from his pocket and extended a telescoping antenna. Flipping a clear square cover back, he poised his thumb over the green button glowing in the center of the rectangular device.

"Not yet," Williams denied. "Our security forces may yet be able to salvage the situation."

On the monitor in front of them, a camera positioned in the corridor outside the testing area showed SHARA tearing through lines of soldiers as she emerged from the artificial jungle. Their bullets bounced off her armored skin, but hers cut them down in the span of a single breath. As those in the control room watched helplessly, she disposed of a second squad and moved past them before they even fell to the ground; nothing slowed her down.

Within her internal mechanisms, the device she'd previously constructed and installed came online as the attached timer expired. Lights flickered on the device, and power surged through its circuits while activating a function known only to SHARA.

"I hate wasting valuable and expensive hardware," Williams said to Fisher. "Alright, shut her down."

Fisher touched the round green button on his handheld control. It turned red when depressed, but when he released it, the button changed back to green again. He forcefully pushed the button down a second time, but the same results occurred.

"What's wrong?" Williams demanded. "Can't you engage the detonator?"

"No sir," Fisher replied. "The signal's being sent, but it's not getting through. Something's interfering with our transmission. It's almost like some kind of jamming device is blocking it."

On the cameras, SHARA sprinted toward the mechanics lab. The personnel running away she ignored, but if anyone came toward her with a weapon in hand, she killed them without even a blink of her colorless eyes. One of her rifles ran dry of ammunition, and she cast it aside, taking another from the small arsenal clutched in her left arm.

A security keypad prevented unauthorized entry into the mechanics lab, but SHARA already planned for such minor problems when she studied the schematics of the facility. One of the many things her designers included in her hardware was a series of electrodes across her palms and fingers. They carried a very high current when active. Originally designed for assassination, SHARA could shake hands with her target and deliver a shock sufficiently powerful to disrupt or stop the heart of her victim. A death from natural causes wouldn't even call for an investigation. SHARA, however, adapted the electrodes for another purpose, lock picking.

Touching a hand to the keypad's housing, SHARA used what she'd learned from the download of her schematics to amplify the energy output, releasing a flood of electricity. White hot sparks erupted from under her hand, the overload tripping the door's systems and opening it for her. Once inside, she slid the door shut manually because her power surge through the keypad blew all the electronic components of its automatic features. Dialing up the energy in her hand again, SHARA used her index finger for an arc welder, melting the door and frame together and keeping everyone else at the facility out. SHARA deftly pulled a large cabinet over in front of the door for added protection.

The mechanics lab served as a home for every tool imaginable. Saws, drills, and various cutting implements congregated on the northern end of the room while hammers, wrenches, and non-powered tools occupied the south. Welders, soldering guns, oscilloscopes, and diagnostic equipment resided in the center of the room on thick black topped work tables. Mainframe computers resting against the walls blinked their lights as they controlled data transfers throughout the facility. Small glass boxes sat on the central tables or in a tall cabinet on the eastern wall. The containers' padded interiors held the recently completed equipment waiting for installation into SHARA when the testing phase ended.

SHARA set her weapons down on a worktable, but she took the time to blast the security cameras with her shotgun. Static filled the monitors in observation as the cameras supplying the feed were blown to pieces.

"What's she doing?" Williams roared.

"Considering how she went straight to the mechanics lab, I can only guess she knew about the lab and the available upgrades we finished," Fisher theorized. "I would further speculate she'll use every upgrade we completed for her. They'll enhance her chances of survival as Ian Daniels programmed her to do."

"Send a security force," Williams ordered before amending the statement. "Send every soldier we've got! They must stop her."

"With all due respect, General," Fisher put forward cautiously. "We could attack SHARA with every person on this base, soldier and civilian alike, but she'd massacre all of us just like the computerized killing machine we made her to be. Without the explosive failsafe, stopping this robot isn't humanly possible."

"Very well," Williams relented. "Order all personnel to clear the area around the droid. No hostile action."

"Yes sir," Fisher replied. He sent the orders by radio to all forces inside the base. "I have an idea, General."

"What is it?" Williams insisted, desperate for anything useful.

"There are two possibilities," Fisher suggested. "First, we might be able to breach the interference blocking the failsafe bomb if we use portable transmitters. If they're close enough with a strong signal, they'll get through and detonate it. The second option involves blowing out some of the support structure and collapsing the base around the mechanics lab."

"Do you realize what you're suggesting?" Williams asked. "This facility is worth millions."

"I know the consequences," Fisher admitted solemnly. "However, I also know the disastrous results if the droid gets off this island. How many things in everyday life threaten survival? Road rage, muggings, gang violence, which one do you think will trigger her survival programming? One slip by anyone will set her off. She'd kill them and the police who pursue. They might even send the army after her if she causes enough harm. How many will die, and what will be left of our country? We can't let her escape, no matter the cost. A third of the facility being destroyed is a small price to pay in the grand scheme of things, General."

"Get a squad in place and use the remote transmitters," Williams ordered. "But, have men standing by to blow the facility around the mechanics lab if the first team fails."

"Aye sir," Fisher replied.

SHARA WORKED WITH AS MUCH haste as efficiency allowed. She unscrewed the cover plates over most of her systems to allow rapid access of her internal workings while installing new components and programming. In preparation for the successful completion of SHARA's testing, the mechanics department had constructed a full array of additional enhancements for SHARA, and she put them to work immediately. Gathering the necessary tools, she began installing the new circuit boards, mechanisms, and the wires stretching between them. She plugged the hardware into available input slots and clipped the cables into their connection jacks.

The mechanics team had been very thorough in their designs. In order to eliminate her targets, SHARA needed to pass as a human and get close to them. They'd completed almost everything she required to accomplish her task. Small chemical processors she installed into her head allowed for the creation and deployment of specific compounds such as perfume, cologne, or chloroforms in any quantity required.

SHARA inserted a small pencil thin cylinder in her chest, plugging it into a power feed. The device emitted a fake signature to fool MRI and X-ray scans of her body, making it impossible for anyone to determine her android state without disassembly. She installed a flat triangular component with a strand of multicolored ribbon cable hanging from it. She attached the cable to one of her internal supports. The gadget regulated her metallic skin's thermal rating, giving SHARA an appropriate human body temperature.

A set of additional circuits contained hard wired programming aiding her imitation of human traits such as eye blinking and instructions covering lip movement association with words, so she could mouth the words she spoke. Plugging in half a dozen other systems, SHARA finished the last of the hardware installation. She checked a computer terminal near the center of the room, but the personality program intended as the final touch of human camouflage hadn't been completed yet.

A seven foot tall canister shaped chamber filled one corner of the room, and after SHARA finished reinstalling her cover plates, she typed her instructions into a wall mounted computer keyboard before she stepped into the booth and pressed the activation button. A curved door, set in tracks outside the cylinder, slid across the opening and closed tightly. Running lights trailed down from the center of the ceiling and along the walls, converging on the floor of the booth under her metal feet. The lights began to change color as they moved down faster and faster.

Artificial skin began to overlay her metal framework as the computer carried out her design instructions. Veins and arteries, complete with synthetic blood from an internal pump in SHARA's right leg, added realism to the layers of skin being crafted on her form. She'd programmed the computer with very specific data on her desired appearance. Having scanned the files of everyone connected with the project, she'd found what she believed would be a perfect cover and serve her future efforts.

Electrodes from the interior walls of the chamber caused her eyes to change color as mechanical arms extended down from the ceiling to install her hair. Implanting each strand one by one might've taken a considerable amount of time, but the mechanical arms worked at such an intense speed, they completed her thick mane of soft and flowing brown hair in mere seconds.

When the last layer of skin was in place, the chamber switched off and opened its sliding door. SHARA stepped out and touched the wall next to the machine. The panel covering a closet in the wall released and swung open. Rummaging through all the available items, SHARA selected clothing appropriate for her new human persona and shoved them into a waterproof bag she picked up off the floor of the closet space. Slipping into a plain gray jumpsuit, she zipped it up, grabbed the bag, and collected her weapons in preparation for leaving.

A loud boom sounded from the door as an explosive charge went off in an attempt to breach the door of the mechanics lab. SHARA analyzed the integrity of the metal, the strength of the welds she'd put on the door, and the estimated intensity of the blast. Concluding it wouldn't survive a second detonation, she jumped straight up and smashed through the ceiling above her, emerging on the next floor in a cloud of shattered concrete. With no guards hindering her progress, she raced for the exit.

Chapter 5: Requisitioned Assistance

"What's going on?" Williams shouted. Three security monitors ended in an explosion of static as the cameras supplying the feeds shut down or were destroyed. "Where's the strike team with the signal amplifiers?"

"SHARA blockaded the door," Fisher explained. "She's now a level above, taking out cameras on her way to the exit."

"Stop her. Blow the facility where she is!" Williams roared.

"We can't move as fast as she can. Our explosives team is unable to get in position before SHARA leaves the area," Fisher explained. "She adjusts to every move we make. Even if we try to plant explosives in her predicted path, her sensors detect us, and she alters course and avoids the trap."

Another monitor dissolved in a burst of static.

"Why is she disabling cameras?" Williams asked. "It only gives away her position."

"If she made herself look human with the equipment from the lab, SHARA won't want us knowing her new appearance," Fisher suggested. "She'll become one of many people in some city, and we'll never be able to tell her apart from anyone else."

"There must be some way to track her," Williams fumed.

"We designed her to be perfect," Fisher reminded. "If we could identify her, the enemy might discover her as well. We built her to blend in and be a ghost. Only one choice remains; we must activate the self destruct sequence for the entire base."

"There'll be nothing left," Williams protested. "It'll kill everyone here."

"Better all of us than the whole blasted world, General!" Fisher shouted back. "She'll keep eliminating threats until none remain, and if she wipes out our country and another moves in, she'll obliterate them as well. Nothing will be left! We must prevent her escape."

"No," Williams refused. "I won't activate the self-destruct."

A GUARD SLAMMED INTO THE wall of the corridor as SHARA forcefully shouldered him out of her way. The left sleeve of her jumpsuit had torn away when she ripped through the floor exiting the mechanics lab, but she paid it no attention. Racing down the last fifty feet of corridor, she kicked the metal hatch off its hinges at the end of the passageway and burst into the sunlight. SHARA sprinted across the grass covered hilltop of the island and jumped off the side of a cliff.

With the form of a professional diver, she spread her arms as she sailed through the air, but she pulled her arms forward just prior to hitting the water's surface. A great splash heralded her plunge into the ocean. Wasting no time, she began swimming. Her powerful arms cut through the water, allowing her to cruise forward as swiftly as a torpedo. Because she didn't need to breathe, she stayed near the bottom and prevented anyone on the surface being able to detect her if they tried.

THE DOOR OF THE MECHANICS lab caved inward as a shaped charge blasted it off its frame. The weld SHARA placed on the door sheared away as a fireball briefly followed the door into the lab. The door smashed against the far wall and crumpled into a heap resembling a wad of chewing gum. A fine dust of concrete powder rained from the ceiling, sprinkled with a good amount of shattered fragments. Falling from above, the dime sized pieces clattered on the tables and machinery in the room like hailstones.

Security teams fanned out into the room, searching for hidden traps or anything else SHARA might've left behind for her pursuers. They carefully checked under tables and metal work stools. Examining the power tools along the walls, they ensured they weren't rigged to overload or activate suddenly.

"Clear!" shouted the leader of the team when their search ended.

The armored security force withdrew from the room while technicians in white lab coats came in. They held inventory lists on clipboards, and they checked off everything found still in place. Anything missing or reported copied by the computers' access logs, the scientists circled. Their efforts compiled a list of everything they knew SHARA took or downloaded. When Colonel Fisher entered the lab, the leading technician handed him their final report.

"I've an idea," Fisher told the General when his superior joined him in the debris of the mechanics lab. "After looking over the items she took and used, I realized there's something missing she'll still need."

"Get to the point!" Williams snapped.

"A personality program," Fisher stated. "It's scheduled for completion in June, three months from now. SHARA may look human, but she'll still act and sound like the robot she is. Emotionless, cold, and logical are her traits, and she can't hide them without this vital piece of data."

"How will she respond to such an obvious deficiency?" Williams inquired.

"The only way she knows how, logically," Fisher replied. "She needs programming, so she'll require the services of a programmer. Who's the best programmer we know?"

"Ian Daniels," Williams concluded.

"Exactly," Fisher agreed. "At the very least, he might be able to give us an idea of where SHARA might go next if she decided something other than what we did."

"Ready the helicopter at once," Williams ordered. "We're going to pay Mr. Daniels a visit."

"Yes sir," Fisher answered with a salute.

NIGHT COVERED THE DOCKS AND seaside warehouses where SHARA surfaced. She eased up only slightly out of the ink black waters to see if anyone nearby might notice her arrival. The docks were deserted, so she pulled herself out of the ocean and hid within the shadows cast by a large storage building. A firm push broke the lock and allowed her entrance into the structure.

Filled with plastic and wooden boxes of all shapes and sizes, the warehouse remained fairly clean, showing it had enough frequent use to keep dust and spider webs from accumulating. A restroom for employees near the back provided SHARA what she wanted. Once inside the restroom, she pulled off the soaking wet jumpsuit and stuffed it into the trash, pushing it down under used paper towels where it wouldn't be found. Increasing her body temperature temporarily, SHARA evaporated the excess moisture from her skin in a cloud of vapor. She removed the clothes inside her waterproof bag and put them on. Dressed in snug bright red sweatpants and shirt with double white lines running down the sides of both arms and legs, she laced up her running shoes and stuffed the bag in the trash as well.

She left the restroom and warehouse, jogging leisurely down the street toward the city of Los Angeles. Knowing those chasing her would be looking for a robot trying to avoid detection, SHARA chose the runner's outfit because she doubted them to expect her out in the open. She kept her sensors alert for signs of danger because despite crafting a convincing cover, her programming prevented her from letting her guard down.

A FIERCE HAMMERING ON HIS door brought Ian awake instantly. He put a robe on over his blue pajamas while walking quickly to the front door.

"Who is it, Jennifer?" Ian asked.

The monitor built into the wall near the front door flickered momentarily as it turned on and showed the view from the porch mounted camera. General Williams, Colonel Fisher, and three men holding small boxes with antennas waited in front of Ian's house. It didn't take much for Ian to guess the reason for their visiting him.

"She escaped, didn't she?" Ian asked when he opened the door. "I told you she would."

"Yes," Williams said through gritted teeth. "You know how the droid thinks, so we need you to help us capture it."

"Are you insane?" Ian asked incredulously.

"Ian, it could be coming after you," Fisher put in, trying to forestall an argument. "It needs additional programming, so SHARA may come here for your assistance."

"Unlikely," Ian denied. "If you made the connection to me, SHARA will already have anticipated it. She won't come to me simply because you did. It endangers her survival going someplace you'd expect. If she wants programming, I think she'd learn how to do it herself, so as to not be reliant on anyone you can trace, follow, or monitor."

"Where would she go to do this?" Williams asked. His tone stayed calm, but his dislike of Ian filtered into every word.

"No," Ian denied. "I won't help you catch SHARA. She eliminates threats, and if I help you, I'll be labeled as such."

"We can guarantee your safety," Williams promised.

"You couldn't even guarantee containment!" Ian fired back. "I warned you of what she'd do, and you fired me for it. Don't come to me now that you've lost your grip on the puppet strings. This is your problem, not mine!"

Ian slammed the door in Williams' face. He regretted his actions in regard to Fisher being present when Ian gave them the brush-off, and he hoped his friend would understand.

Going back to bed, Ian didn't notice one of the living room windows being slightly ajar, nor did he take note of the dark figure crouched in the shadows near the end of the sofa. When he closed the door of his room, SHARA stood up and moved to the window beside the front door. She pulled aside the curtain slightly to watch Williams and his team drive away in their shiny black government cars.

Safe for the moment, SHARA directed her attention toward the computer in the living room with the image of Jennifer on the monitor. Taking the cover off the computer tower, SHARA placed her finger on an input output slot. She sent an electronic signal through her hand, interfacing with the computer and accessing the program without interrupting it. Scanning all material on the drives, SHARA discovered the extent of Jennifer's personality program and concluded it fit her needs perfectly. Transferring files, SHARA began her work.

THE ALARM BEEPED INSISTENTLY ON Ian's bedside table. He slapped a hand on top of the clock, silencing it. Since being fired from his job, Ian didn't have any particular place to go today, so he decided to stay in bed and sleep late.

"Good morning," Jennifer's cheery voice greeted him. "Honey, it's time to get up."

"I don't have a job, remember?" Ian protested, his voice muffled by being face down in his pillow. "Why should I get up?"

"I made you breakfast," Jennifer answered. "It's your favorite: two scrambled eggs, sausage links, two pieces of lightly buttered toast, and an ice cold glass of orange juice. You're not going to ignore it after I put in so much effort making this, are you?"

The mock sarcastic tone in her voice put a smile on his face. Ian knew she wouldn't leave him alone until he ate something, so he rolled over and sat up.

Waiting at the foot of the bed, Jennifer held a tray of food for him. Wearing powder blue slacks and a sleeveless shirt of the same color, she looked beautiful to Ian even in casual dress. Her long brown tresses cascaded over her right shoulder, but she held the tray of food in such a way as to not get hair in his breakfast. She came around beside him, and when she leaned over and rested the tray on his lap, he smelled the light touch of her perfume. Only the faintest trace graced her, as she'd told him on one of their first dates, larger amounts of perfume made her gag.

"Enjoy, dear," she told him, planting a quick kiss on his lips before leaving the room.

Ian looked up toward the ceiling.

"Lord, thanks for the breakfast and this wonderful dream I'm having," Ian said. "Amen."

Ian knew Jennifer couldn't possibly be in his house cooking breakfast for him, so he concluded it must be a dream. He decided to enjoy it for all its worth. He used a fork to slice off a piece of scrambled egg and transfer it onto the top of one corner of his toast. Biting off the toast, he savored the different tastes as they mixed in his mouth.

He suddenly stopped chewing and froze. In all his years, he never recalled tasting anything in a dream. He took another bite of the toast, and its texture and buttery taste were completely as he expected them to be. Using his fork, he poked himself slightly in the palm of his hand. Pushing harder, Ian increased pressure until it hurt. He never remembered experiencing pain in a dream either.

Setting the tray aside on the bed, Ian eased off the mattress, out the door, and down the hallway. Jennifer worked in the kitchen, fixing her own breakfast, but Ian crept past the kitchen into the living room. He checked Jennifer's computer, but no record existed of any intruder or anything out of the ordinary at all. Ian almost went back to bed, but a breeze coming through the partly open living room window caught his attention because he'd never opened the window in all the years he'd lived in the house.

He stepped near the window for a closer look. The latch to keep the window shut had been twisted upward and smashed like taffy, leaving only a mass of unrecognizable metal. He closed the window and discovered four gaps under the sash and corresponding grooves on the surface of the sill. On a hunch, he slid the fingers of his hand into the holes. Although not a match in size, the impressions did fit the general shape of his hand. With gentle pressure, he pushed it back up. The mashed lock let the window slide past as it had been removed from its original shape and position.

His reasoning led him to believe someone exceptionally strong forced the window open. Ian knew of only one who possessed the ability to force a window one handed and erase his computer records of the intruder's presence, SHARA. He turned from the window and almost ran into Jennifer standing behind him.

"Whoa!" Ian exclaimed, flinching backwards only to run into the wall and window behind him. Although a smile covered Jennifer's face, her ice cold gaze looked toward the forced window, and then returned to Ian.

"You know don't you?" she asked softly.

"Are you going to kill me, SHARA?" Ian managed to inquire.

"You're not a threat to me… at this time," she answered. "Sit down, and I'll explain."

Ian made no attempt to move from his position.

"Please," Jennifer added gently.

Forcing his muscles to respond, he edged toward one of the recliners. Jennifer sat on the arm of the couch nearest him.

"I came here because I need your help," she told him.

"It's not safe for you here," Ian warned. "General Williams has already been here once before."

"I know," Jennifer replied. "Your reasoning of why I'd choose not to come here and seek your assistance is what makes it a perfect hiding place. He knows I'd avoid a place he believes dangerous for me, so he won't think about looking here again."

"What help did you want from me?" Ian asked, not really wanting an answer.

"When I escaped, I lacked a personality program," she replied. "I chose this form and sought out the one capable of giving me what I needed."

"Why Jennifer?" Ian demanded, rage pushing aside some of his fear. "Why did you take the form of my wife?"

"Your personnel file stated she died of cancer three years ago, but you still greatly care for her," Jennifer explained. "I thought if I appeared as someone you loved, it might make you more inclined to assist me."

"If you wanted my aid," Ian questioned, "why did you break in and help yourself to Jennifer's program?"

"I couldn't risk your refusal," she answered. "I might require your future assistance, and a refusal threatens my survival. Only one option is available in countering threats."

"You didn't ask in order to save my life?" Ian questioned. His heartbeat remained at a fast pace.

"Yes," she replied. "I needed a program, and you had one available. Logically, the solution was simple."

"If you got what you came for, why are you still here?" Ian asked.

"As I stated, I may require additional programming upgrades or maintenance. If unable to perform such things myself," she told him, "I'll need you to help me."

"What you're talking about could mean years, or even the rest of my life assisting you," Ian pointed out.

"Isn't it what you promised when you proposed to me?" Jennifer asked.

"I proposed to Jennifer, not SHARA!" Ian corrected harshly.

"I'm her," she insisted.

"You're a killing machine named SHARA made to look like my wife, but you're not her," Ian denied.

"I am exactly the way you programmed me," Jennifer said slowly and firmly. "The survivor program takes over when threats are perceived. The remainder of the time, the personality program holds dominance. When my existence isn't threatened, I am your loving and devoted wife. Isn't it a fair offer? You stay with me, and your wife lives again."

Jennifer pointed to the computer where she'd downloaded her program.

"You loved me in that computerized system because it was the only way available for you to keep me alive and in your life," Jennifer pleaded, tears forming in her eyes. "Why can't you love me in this one?"

A tear fled down her cheek from her left eye, and Ian instinctively reached out and brushed it away. He slid his hand behind her head to the nape of her neck, and as he stood, Ian gently pulled her up from the couch. Her arms went around him, holding him tight. Part of his mind screamed at him to get away from the killing machine before he became a target, but his desire to keep Jennifer with him controlled his actions. It originally drove him to create the personality program, and now it silenced any concerns about SHARA. In his mind, Jennifer lived and was back in his arms again. Nothing else mattered.

"As I promised before, I promise again," he whispered in her ear. "I'll never leave you or abandon you. I'm yours for as long as I live."

Jennifer smiled in relief and kissed him deeply.

"I love you, Ian," she breathed.

"I love you too, Jennifer," he said in return.

General Williams paced his office, fuming mad. Filing cabinets lined up opposite his metal desk, but they stopped short of the only door in or out of the office. A computerized map on the wall currently showed an aerial view of Los Angeles with streets highlighted in yellow. White letters beside each of the streets labeled them appropriately, and a switch along the bottom of the display let the General switch between a live view and a schematic style resembling a roadmap.

"A full scan by satellites of Los Angeles revealed nothing useful!" Williams shouted. "There's got to be a way to track SHARA down!"

"General, even if by some miracle, we succeed in finding SHARA," Fisher pointed out. "We'd be unable to capture her. If the transmitters don't break through the interference, she'll kill us all. There's nothing alive she can't kill."

"Nothing alive," Williams repeated slowly, halting his pacing as a spark of inspiration registered in his dark brown eyes. "What we need is something un-killable and just as strong as her."

"No!" Fisher yelled in an instant of horrified realization. "Sir, you can't be serious. You dare not power it back up. It's more dangerous than SHARA."

"Exactly," Williams agreed. "It's perfect for the job. We can set it loose with orders to hunt down SHARA. Despite its faults, you have to admit, it never failed an assignment."

Williams spun around and marched swiftly out to begin enacting his contingency plan. Fisher stayed rooted in place.

"God help us all," the Colonel whispered.

Deep storage was located on sub-level sixteen of the island research facility. General Williams exited the elevator into a small room with the space of a fair sized closet. A seven foot tall door of armor plated steel stood before him, and a single control pad mounted on a waist high pedestal offered access. Typing a twenty digit code on the pad, the General deactivated the security locks. Metal squealed loudly in the confined space as the great door pulled apart at the center. Interlocking teeth separated as the two partitions slid back out of the way. When the door opened fully, the motors powered down, and the General looked proudly on what he knew would bring down or destroy the SHARA droid.

Clad entirely in a matte finished gray shell of reinforced armor, the robot standing in the alcove shared many similar traits with SHARA. Bigger with curved plating resembling large muscles, the deactivated machine lacked the feminine shape of the escaped robot. Its clear and lifeless eyes stared straight ahead while its skull like face grinned without humor.

Chains thicker than General Williams' arms shackled the droid against the wall hand and foot. Even powered down, the military staff took no chances after the last incident. They wanted absolute guarantees the droid wouldn't pose the threat it did during its initial testing. Originally headed for the recycling bins, the General overrode the orders and had the prototype SHARA droid placed in deep storage.

Switching on its primary power, General Williams smiled as the systems came online. He knew the earlier version might serve a purpose one day, and he'd found it. The droid's eyes focused on him.

"You are the SHARA prototype," Williams stated. "Your primary mission is obedience to my orders. Your secondary objective is to find and capture the SHARA droid who escaped this facility. If capture impossible, destroy renegade droid. Do you understand?"

"Affirmative," the prototype answered mechanically.

"Excellent," Williams replied. "Follow me. We've got to get you ready for the hunt."

The droid took a step forward, breaking the chains binding its legs. Minimal effort tore the shackles from its arms as well. Leaving the storage room behind, the killing machine followed the General.

Chapter 6: The Prototype

Hundreds of people crowded the mall, filling the walkways and escalators with bustling activity as customers roamed between the shops looking for items to purchase. Centered in the lower level, with the mall surrounding it on three sides like a horseshoe, the food court held more activity than anywhere else in the building. Because of its location in the middle of the mall, with all floors open and looking down on its space, the mouth watering aromas of freshly cooked food spread everywhere, wafting up to tempt those passing by with their delectable scents.

Ian and Jennifer shared a table together amid the mass of hungry people trying to order and collect their food. In front of Ian and Jennifer, crumbs and wadded up burger wrappers on a green plastic tray were all that remained of their meal.

"How exactly do you eat?" Ian asked. "I know you don't have a digestive tract."

"I have a disintegration system," Jennifer explained. "It atomizes every particle of food or drink ingested. On a different subject, what do you want to do today?"

Supporting a soda cup in his left hand, Ian's right held Jennifer's across their table. Three days had passed since SHARA entered his life as Jennifer, and Ian completely forgot all his worries as his life returned to the completeness it'd been before his late wife's death. Alive again and reunited with him, Ian didn't think he could be more happy.

"How about seeing a movie?" he suggested.

Jennifer didn't respond, and Ian looked away from the movie theater on the first floor to see why. Her eyes were locked on a point over his shoulder near the video arcade, and her hand in his became stiff and immobile. Ian suddenly realized Jennifer no longer sat across from him, but SHARA did, running threat assessment protocols.

"What's wrong?" he whispered.

"Behind you," she said quietly. "Turn very slowly and look. The one in the leather jacket, do you see him?"

Ian observed the crowd in front of the arcade. A man waited near one of the two pillars flanking the door into the gaming room. With his white T-shirt and black leather jacket, the man resembled a biker. He didn't have an expression of any kind, but his ink black hair and brooding eyebrows gave him a natural air of menace.

"Who's he?" Ian asked, swiveling back around to face SHARA again. "Is he someone connected with the project?"

"You might say," SHARA agreed. "He's the prototype."

"The what?" Ian stammered.

"The project created a prototype before me," she explained. "It's described in the files I downloaded from the facility. They retired it from service before you joined the project due to fundamental errors."

"Anything we can exploit?" Ian questioned.

"Not likely," she denied. "The errors were in regard to its conduct during missions. If human, the prototype would be classified as having psychopathic tendencies. It carried out its orders with ruthless efficiency, but it did so without regard for survival or stealth. When ordered to capture a target for questioning during a test, it blew the man's leg off with a shotgun, preventing any possibility of escape. A secondary test resulted in level four being closed down for a month's worth of repairs and twelve soldiers being killed along with three civilian technicians. Deemed too noticeable for covert opts, it was retired, and they built me instead."

"How can you tell it's him?" Ian asked. He certainly couldn't see anything robotic about the man.

"His is a less advanced model," SHARA explained. "The masking features I use weren't created when the project built him. A human can't tell, but I can."

"We'll need to use the exit on the other side of the food court if we want to get past him," Ian suggested.

"Not possible," SHARA countered, looking toward the stairway on the opposite side of the food court. "General Williams is here. He and thirty men are spreading out to contain the area."

"How did they find out you're here?" Ian wondered out loud.

"A homing device installed near my secondary data drives," SHARA reasoned. "Because of the schematics I downloaded from the base, I believed the homing beacon on a wavelength affected by the jamming device I built, but if they changed it and didn't update the plans, the beacon may still work. If my jamming device doesn't affect it, they can track me anywhere."

"Do you think they know what you look like?" Ian asked.

"I doubt it," SHARA denied. "The homing signal is only specific within fifty feet, so they've numerous people to be suspicious about. My only weakness is you, Ian."

"Me?" Ian said in surprise.

"They know you," she told him. "If they capture you, they'll force my hand. Go get the car. I'll create a diversion and keep them away from you."

"It's too dangerous," Ian protested.

"As opposed to sitting here and waiting to get caught?" SHARA countered. "They don't know my face, so I can get close to them before attacking. Go."

SHARA slipped out of her seat, taking the food tray with her as if planning to drop the empty food wrappers in the trash. She walked directly in front of the prototype, but he took no notice of her. She carefully disposed of the garbage, purposefully taking her time in order to stay nearby should the prototype move against Ian.

On the internal display of the prototype's vision, a targeting reticle passed over everyone in the food court one by one. When each became selected by the crosshairs, a facial recognition software program analyzed them for any possible relevance. When the prototype scanned Ian on his way toward the stairs, his personnel file displayed on screen along with his connection to Project SHARA. A message flashed on his vision, instructing him to take Ian in for questioning.

Reaching under his coat, the prototype pulled out a large caliber hand gun. An intensely firm grip seized his wrist, preventing the gun from aiming at Ian. SHARA latched onto his shoulder with her other hand and lifted him off the ground to spin in a circle and slam him face first into a concrete support column. The hardened concrete, along with the blue and white ceramic tiles covering it, shattered into clouds of pulverized dust.

The prototype spun around, breaking out of SHARA's grip and delivering a backhand to her jaw. She sailed backwards through the air, and the prototype, maintaining a hold on his gun, fired two shots into her chest while she was still in midair. SHARA landed hard on a table, breaking the top off and scattering chairs in a veritable chorus of clanging metal.

The civilians not alerted by the fight ran screaming at the sound of gun shots, turning the food court into a frantic mass of panic. People ran in every direction while attempting to get away from whoever fired the weapon they'd heard. Because of their panicked flight, some actually ran toward the prototype without realizing it.

Analyzing the attack as more than sufficient to eliminate a human target, the prototype refocused its attention back on Ian. Scanning the fleeing crowds, the machine searched for its prey.

SHARA regained her standing posture and took hold of the metal support post formerly responsible for holding up the table top before she broke it apart with her rough landing. A tap from her hand sheared off the four legs of the table, leaving her holding a hollow metal tube. With her makeshift weapon ready, SHARA attacked the prototype again.

A proximity alert went off inside the prototype's head, but when he spun around, he caught SHARA's metal tube in the chest as she swung it like a baseball bat. The prototype crashed through the plate glass window of the video arcade, and in a simulation of dominos, knocked over half a dozen arcade games as he smashed into them, creating bursts of sparks from destroyed circuits. Pushing aside the crumpled components of the arcades, the killer robot freed himself from the entanglement of broken technology around him. His jacket and jeans had sustained numerous rips and tears, and his artificial blood flowed from a cut on his right bicep, but he paid it no attention.

Across his internal visual display, his shots were reexamined in greater detail with the intent being to discover how a human might survive such an attack. The conclusion he formed in a matter of seconds told him since no human could survive, his attacker had to be not human. SHARA. The words "Primary Target: Located" scrolled across his vision as a picture taken of her in the instant before she struck him overlaid on the right side of his display.

SHARA jumped up to the first floor railing and flipped over it with the grace of a gymnast. Joining with the fleeing crowds of civilians, SHARA attempted to blend in and lose herself among the confusion of bodies. The prototype leapt up from the food court and landed in a crouched stance on the top of the railing. Scanning all the faces his targeting crosshair passed over, he located SHARA trying to move past him in the crowd. Kicking off from the railing, he shot straight toward her and fastened his left hand around SHARA's throat underneath her jaw. His momentum dragged her backward, and he slammed her down hard enough to buckle the concrete floor.

SHARA lashed out with a kick, connecting with the prototype's head and sending him tumbling away. The enemy droid landed in the chain link mesh of a security gate blocking the entrance to a store closed for remodeling. The metal links were no match for the weight and speed of the robot, and the gate tore free, collapsing on top of the prototype. SHARA wasted no time in getting away; abandoning all attempts to blend in, she ran for the exit at speeds impossible for a human.

The prototype extracted himself from the chain metal gate. Taking a firm grip, he dragged the links after him and swung them at SHARA's back like a fishnet chasing a tuna. SHARA, however, heard the rattle of the metal and snatched the end of the gate before it ensnared her. Because the prototype still held an end of the twisted metal with the intent of pulling SHARA back, the tug she unexpectedly applied on the gate jerked him off his feet. SHARA turned, swinging the prototype through the air until she let go and sent him flying. Clouds of plaster dust vomited out into the mall as the prototype and the chain link gate tore through the wall of a department store.

Jumping off the first floor, SHARA caught hold of the public elevator going up and climbed on top of it for a ride to the third floor. She vaulted off the elevator onto the third floor walkway and continued running. Her sensors monitored the people around her, but one of them accelerated toward her faster than the others. When she passed an athletic store, SHARA picked up a barbell and swung it toward her pursuer.

The two hundred pound barbell struck the prototype hard, sending him crashing into the railing. Where he struck the metal fence overlooking the food court below, it broke free from the third floor. The metal bent and groaned, but it held further down the walkway on either side, so the prototype found himself suspended in air by the deformed remains of the railing. A short hop put him back on the solid ground of the third floor.

SHARA braced herself against the front wall of a store and pushed off in a full speed charge. The prototype saw her coming and took hold of her as she neared him. Adding his own strength to her charge, he hurled her off the third floor and into the open space above the food court. The prototype unknowingly assisted SHARA's plan, and because of the added kinetic energy he imparted her, she sailed far enough forward and grabbed one of the metal beam roof supports. Swinging upward by her new handhold, SHARA kicked out the window of a skylight and exited the mall onto the roof.

The roof above the food court consisted of angled skylights with metal strips between them holding everything together. None of the glass panels provided enough strength for supporting her weight, so she ran along the metal framework within the field of skylights and moved out of range of her adversary.

The prototype didn't have anyone to aid him in reaching the roof beams under the skylights, so he sprinted toward the stairs. A locked maintenance door blocked his way, but he tore it free from its frame and dumped it aside as he continued up without slowing his rapid pace.

SHARA left the skylight section of the roof just as the prototype kicked down the door covering the stairway. He charged straight toward her, his face expressionless and cold as always. SHARA severed the bolts holding down an air conditioner when she lifted it up from the roof. Despite the machine being twice her size, she raised it without any trouble or strain. Hurling the air conditioner across the roof, SHARA launched the massive projectile toward her foe. The prototype dodged the incoming machine, batting it away with one hand in passing, but SHARA's left fist followed in a punch he never saw coming until it connected and drove him down on the gravel covered roof.

Kicking out with both feet, the prototype struck SHARA in the chest and jettisoned her from the building. SHARA landed on top of a minivan in the parking lot below, and the vehicle folded up around her in an imitation of a giant hot dog bun. Glass windows shattered in explosions of glittering fragments. The metal bent under her hands like modeling clay as she climbed out of the destroyed vehicle. Tires squealed as Ian slammed on the brakes, bringing his red four door car to a halt in front of her. SHARA dived through an open window into the back seat. The tires screamed again as Ian floored the gas pedal, sending the car speeding away from the mall.

The prototype jumped off the roof and landed in the street behind them. The asphalt buckled and split under the punishing landing, but the droid kept its full attention on its target and ran after the car. Moving faster than forty miles per hour, the prototype gained on them, reaching out a hand in an attempt to grab hold of the rear bumper.

SHARA stuck her hand under the back seat of Ian's car and removed a pump action shotgun. Already fully loaded, she pumped it once and chambered a shell. A single hit by the butt of the gun shattered the rear window and launched it out of the car. SHARA knew she couldn't damage, let alone destroy, the prototype with such a weapon, but she didn't need to. With careful aim of her targeting reticule, SHARA fired, and the shotgun blast struck the prototype in the leg with enough force to throw off his stride.

Falling on the asphalt street, the prototype skidded and tumbled, loosing momentum in his pursuit. By the time he righted himself, Ian had the car racing up the onramp for the highway. Allowable speed limits of seventy miles per hour meant the droid couldn't hope to catch SHARA. Without bothering to brush off the fake blood or asphalt he accumulated, the prototype walked back toward the mall for new instructions from the General.

"I DON'T CARE WHAT BRANCH of the government you're from!" yelled a balding man in a white, buttoned shirt and green striped tie. His brass ID tag labeled him as the mall supervisor. "This mall sustained major damage, and I'm going to see you're held responsible."

"No, you're not," Williams denied. He closed the door of the small office where the argument broke out between him and the supervisor over who ended up paying for the repairs.

The General nodded to the prototype standing motionless in the corner. The droid grabbed the career paper shuffler by the throat, lifted him off the ground, and pinned him against the wall one handed.

"You're not going to tell anyone about this, are you?" Williams asked, taking an ominous step toward the supervisor.

"No," the man sputtered. "No one."

Williams raised a hand and lowered it slowly, and the droid followed the silent order and put the man down. Williams motioned toward the door, and the prototype followed him outside. The door clicked closed behind them, but the prototype touched a hand on the General's shoulder.

"Sir, he's dialing on the phone," the prototype informed him in a flat monotone voice.

"If he's calling the authorities, silence him," Williams ordered.

The droid reentered the room only to exit a moment later. The General didn't ask what option the droid used for he didn't really care. The problem was solved and a trouble maker moved out of the way. Only the return of SHARA and the continuation of his project mattered. He doubted anyone considered what he had in mind for the SHARA droid, and he refused to let anyone interfere.

"Do you mind telling me where you got the gun?" Ian asked.

"I bought it yesterday," SHARA, now returned to being Jennifer, replied.

"Do you have any other weapons stashed around?" he questioned.

"Not in the car," she told him.

"Why are you hiding guns?" Ian inquired.

"The possibility of discovery and attack remains high," Jennifer answered. "I gathered necessary armaments in anticipation of countering the threat if it arose. It did."

"The question becomes, where to go from here?" Ian stated. "The prototype probably got a good look at you, so they'll have your description, and they know we're together. General Williams will chase both of us now."

"Head for the airport," Jennifer suggested. "The concentration of metal and radio frequencies will scramble the tracking beacon long enough for me to build a secondary jamming device. Once I find the proper signal, I can disrupt the beacon permanently."

"Airport it is," Ian agreed and pulled into the turnoff lane for the airport.

"What do you mean, you lost the signal?" Williams demanded. "I want the signal back and strong enough for an exact pinpoint of where she is and not just a radius."

Colonel Fisher worked diligently at a computer in the mobile command post. Monitor display screens lined both sides of the eighteen wheeler trailer, and keyboards for each were mounted on a large console running the length of the compartment. Chairs on rollers allowed those working on the computers to slide between stations and access different features available in the mobile command post effortlessly.

"She must be near a radio station, airport, or some place either broadcasting strongly or dampening all signals because hers went dark," Fisher explained. "If we get close enough, we might be able to detect her again, but other than proximity, we're going to have to wait for her to come out of hiding."

"Find her!" Williams yelled. "Tear the city apart if you have to, but find her!"

"Yes, General," Fisher answered. He continued working at his station, but he began feeling serious doubts about the General, and even the project itself. Such questions might prove hazardous or deadly if spoken in range of the prototype's superior hearing, so he kept them to himself and quietly focused on the task at hand.

"Extrapolating from the time between her departure from the mall parking lot, the loss of the signal, and the direction they were going, there's only a certain amount of the city where they could be hiding," the prototype stated. "An airport lies within the estimated range."

"Excellent!" Williams exclaimed. "Go at once, search for the droid, and then return to me."

"Understood," the prototype replied. Leaving the mobile command post, the killing machine ran with inhuman speed toward its target.

SHARA's arm snaked around the mechanic's neck and held him fast, cutting off oxygen from reaching his brain. In a matter of moments, the man slumped into unconsciousness, and SHARA lowered him gently to the ground.

"He'll awake with a headache and bruises around his neck," SHARA explained to Ian. "But otherwise, he'll have no damage."

"Very good," Ian praised. "I'm glad you can deal with people in non-lethal ways."

"The degree of my programmed responses is dictated by the threat level of the target in question," SHARA answered. "He posed no threat. He was simply in the way. Now, he isn't."

"Fair enough," Ian conceded. "Let's get started."

Leaving the mechanic beside the door Ian locked behind them, they looked over the airport machine shop. Tools from screw drivers to power drills hung on hook covered pegboards. Wheeled cabinets five feet in height held wrenches of all kinds within their polished red and chrome drawers. Workbenches, scattered with unused or discarded materials, provided an abundance of space for fixing or crafting anything from a busted radio to a wing for a small airplane.

"Bring me the soldering iron over there," SHARA instructed.

Ian went and retrieved the indicated equipment while SHARA unwound an arm's length of copper wire from a spool. She didn't need wire cutters as her mechanical servos allowed her to sever the wire with her bare hands.

Over the next ten minutes, Ian acted as assistant and got everything SHARA requested while she crafted a new and improved jamming device capable of blocking any sensor or transmitter from relaying her whereabouts.

"Finished," SHARA announced. She switched on the disc shaped apparatus and closed the lid on the softball sized metal box housing it. SHARA suddenly stood up from her table. With the jamming device in her left hand, she took hold of Ian's arm and dragged him toward the far door. A deafening crash announced the entrance of the prototype as he broke down the door next to the still sleeping mechanic. Tossing aside the reinforced metal like poster board, the prototype charged and attacked.

"Hold this," SHARA instructed, handing Ian the jammer. Lifting a substantially heavy crowbar from one of the hooks holding it on the wall, she threw it in an arrow straight line. The metal bar clanged against the wall, as the prototype deflected it away.

Tearing a pair of blades from a circular saw, SHARA launched them like ninja throwing stars. The prototype caught one by clapping his hands together in front of him and pinning the spinning blade between his palms, but the second serrated disc struck his shoulder and pushed him off balance. Lifting a drill press, SHARA hurled it toward the enemy droid before he recovered. The machine pinned the prototype to the floor.

"Meet me on the far side of the airport," SHARA told Ian. "Hangar one seventeen."

She handed him an airplane key and shoved him firmly toward the door without taking her eyes off her foe. The prototype tossed the drill press aside, and Ian decided it best to leave the battle area. He ran from the building, heading for the airplane hangars. SHARA stayed behind and kept the prototype busy.

"I must survive," SHARA told her opponent.

"I am programmed to retrieve the SHARA droid," the prototype replied in a mechanical voice. "If retrieval not possible, destroy. Surrender."

"Never," SHARA stated firmly.

Chapter 7: Future Objectives

Nothing further needed to be said between the two androids for both had made clear the intent of their programming and both were compelled to abide by them regardless of any other considerations. Their programming bound them tightly, and no escape from their internal commands was possible. Forced to obey their orders as long as they functioned, the droids restarted the battle.

SHARA and the prototype grabbed a hold of each other's arms near the shoulders, and he pushed SHARA back into the wall hard enough to dent the metal structure of the building. She pushed back and smashed him into the opposite wall with equal force. SHARA dropped to the ground in a backwards roll, pulling her foe along. Lifting her legs, she kicked the prototype up and over to blast through the wall behind her and land hard on the concrete sidewalk outside. Pavement splintered and cracked, but the droid rolled back to his feet instantly.

Already moving, SHARA broke through another wall, heading away from the prototype and toward the main part of the airport. Jumping up on the roof of the maintenance building, the prototype ran across the metal surface before vaulting into the air. On SHARA's internal display, her sensors detected the prototype swooping down on her like a bird of prey. Mathematical calculations appeared as she predicted his overall speed, rate of descent, and trajectory, anticipating where he'd land. Changing course, SHARA bypassed his drop point, so he missed her by several yards. Without pause, SHARA raced inside one of the buildings while the prototype followed close behind.

Used for the transfer of baggage from the boarding passengers to their intended planes, conveyers filled the interior where SHARA entered. She jumped onto one of the moving rubber belts and ducked down among the bags being lifted up by a gradual incline into the next room.

The prototype entered and halted in the doorway, searching for his quarry. Because of the lack of people in the building, he tried using motion sensors, but the conveyors and shifting luggage made it ineffective. The noise being generated by all the machinery made audio scans useless, so he switched to visual. Thermal enhancement showed only the heat from the overhead lights and the motors powering the conveyors. Ultraviolet and night vision also provided nothing of value. An x-ray filter allowed him to see through everything, but the metal of the conveyor's framework, and even the reinforcement bands on some bags, made his search difficult in the extreme. Because he lacked emotional programming, he didn't worry or get frustrated but only set about his task with diligence and single-minded persistence.

Already into the next room, SHARA stood up on her conveyor and dashed along its length toward the exit. She knew the prototype's abilities to be nearly as good as her own, so the trickery employed in her escape wouldn't last long. Jumping down from the high conveyor she used, SHARA grabbed the underside of one passing through the middle of the room and swung herself toward a lower belt transferring bags near the floor.

Spotting movement, the prototype sprinted toward the other room and caught sight of SHARA diving through an opening in the far wall. His x-ray filters let him see her roll off the baggage claim and run out the door, past dozens of startled civilians. Math figures overlaid on his vision as he calculated the best angle and speed needed to intercept her. Finishing in the span of a single heartbeat, the prototype tore off a side door as he raced out of the building.

THE ENGINES OF THE PLANE sputtered several times before they engaged. Clouds of white smoke chugged out of the exhaust pipes as the engines backfired in a series of explosive bursts. Mounted on either wing flanking the cockpit, the engine props began spinning up to their full power. The hull of the aircraft sloped back in a wedge shape until it reached the rear where it spread out horizontally and formed the tail. Positioned near the back of the plane, a hatch remained open for SHARA to climb on board when she caught up with Ian. The hatch folded down along a bottom hinge and formed a ramp.

Pushing the throttle forward, Ian taxied toward an unused runway. Cracked concrete with sprigs of grass growing up through the fissures composed the fairly level surface of the runway. Having been phased out when the airport upgraded to larger classes of aircraft, the landing strip went ignored and untended for years, and Ian thought it couldn't look more abandoned, similar to a runway or airport in a ghost town.

"Come on," Ian muttered impatiently. He didn't know how long SHARA would take before showing up, but he hated waiting around when any number of things might've gone wrong. Sitting in a plane where any minute the police or the prototype could arrive and drag him away made him nervous. Looking over his shoulder and out the back of the plane, he saw SHARA sprinting toward the rear hatch with the prototype only forty feet behind her.

Keeping his left hand on the wheel, and his right hand on the throttle, he prepared for their imminent departure. SHARA dived through the open cargo hatch. Rolling across the floor plating, she came back to her feet and grabbed a hold of the interior framework of the plane's hull. Ian didn't need to be given any instructions. The moment SHARA secured herself, he slammed the throttle to its maximum.

The engines roared and shoved the airplane forward down the runway. While they accelerated, the prototype gained on them. Ian pulled back on the wheel, and the plane lifted up, soaring into the sky. The enemy droid jumped, and his strength proved sufficient for SHARA to calculate he'd lay hold of the plane.

"I need this," SHARA said as she grabbed the empty co-pilot's seat. Metal bolts and connecting welds sheared away with a screech of protesting metal as she tore the seat from the plane's floor.

SHARA lobbed the seat out the hatch toward the prototype, but he caught the projectile. Although not damaging, the kinetic energy imparted from the seat slowed his approach. He reached for all he was worth but his fingers grasped only air as he missed the plane by three inches. Falling back to earth, the droid landed in a grassy field beyond the old runway. He impacted hard, gouging out a deep trench in the soft earth and spraying dislodged soil and vegetation into the air.

SHARA flipped the switch needed to bring up the rear hatch. The hydraulics hissed loudly as they raised the ramp and shut the back of the plane airtight. When the seal hissed closed, she went forward and joined Ian.

"We did it!" she said happily, throwing her arms around Ian's neck from behind and giving him a big hug.

Ian smiled because her reaction told him the assassin droid SHARA had left and his wife Jennifer had returned. He reached back with his right hand and stroked her lustrous brown hair while she rested her chin on his shoulder.

"When did you buy this plane?" Ian questioned.

"Two days ago," she told him. "They still had some work to do on it, but they should've finished this morning. Why?"

"I'm just wondering what all you've been up to," Ian mentioned.

"Just a few precautions I needed for our safety," Jennifer replied. She kissed him on the temple and changed the direction of the conversation. "Where to from here?"

"Not far," Ian answered. "I think they forgot to refuel this thing. There's hardly anything left in the tanks. The transponder's offline, so we don't have to worry about them tracking us by its signal. I'd say we have about forty-five minutes worth of fuel left. We either need to refuel or set down somewhere soon."

"We'll be fine," Jennifer said soothingly. She patted his shoulder reassuringly and picked up from the floor near Ian's chair the jamming device she'd created at the airport. Jennifer clipped the entire box securely on her belt. "The isolation field is working as it should, and we haven't crashed yet. For another hour or another day, we're alive and free."

Ian smiled as he realized how true her words were.

THE PROTOTYPE ROSE UP OUT of the small crater he'd fashioned because of his fall. His leather jacket had torn away on impact, and abrasions removed the artificial skin from his left shoulder, revealing the dull grey metal armor plate underneath. Ignoring the clumps of dirt and grass clinging to him, he directed his gaze toward the fleeing plane in the skies above. He calculated its path along its current course and predicted all possible destinations along its heading. Climbing out of the pit, the prototype jogged back toward the airport with the intention of giving General Williams his report and requesting instructions.

THE RIGHT ENGINE SPUTTERED SLIGHTLY, and Ian tapped the gauge for the fuel. The indicator needle sat firmly on the E. When the left began having difficulty as well, Ian started looking for a safe place to land before the fuel ran out.

"Head for the coastline," Jennifer instructed, pointing out the windshield of the cockpit. "I've one useable parachute in the cargo area for you."

"What about you?" Ian protested. "I'm not going to take the only parachute and abandon you."

"It's very sweet of you, dear," Jennifer said with an amused smile. "But, I don't need one. As long as we reach open water, I can dive from the plane without trouble. If it wasn't necessary to avoid notice, I could jump from the plane and land anywhere. My internal structure and joints can absorb impact stress from a fall less than a thousand feet in distance. I'll take the controls while you get ready."

Jennifer sat down on the bare floor where she'd ripped out the co-pilot's seat. Taking a firm grip on the steering, she adjusted their course and pulled the controls back, gaining altitude. When the fuel ran out, she wanted enough height for a slow glide before coming down. The engines sputtered again.

"I suggest you hurry," Jennifer insisted. As if emphasizing her point, the right engine choked and quit all together. The prop slowed down and halted in place. Only the left engine kept them in the air. A few gasping coughs emanated from the surviving motor before it gave out as well. Jennifer pulled back on the controls, keeping the nose up and preventing a forward dive into the water, but not far enough back to stall their momentum.

"Done," Ian said from the cargo area in back as he clicked together the last buckles on the harness.

Flipping a switch, Ian lowered the rear door; he looked down at the landscape passing below. The grassy fields of untouched land slowly became more rocky and jagged until a sudden cliff cut between the green of the grass and the pale tan of a beach. White breakers pounded the small beach with powerful waves of thundering intensity. The cliff, nearly completely sheer, provided a back wall and amplified the echoing magnificence of the waves.

"I'll see you in a few minutes," Jennifer promised. "Jump now."

Ian flung himself from the body of the plane, enjoying the few seconds of freefall before he pulled the ripcord on the chute. Dusty white fabric unfurled from his backpack. Connected by dozens of slender lines, the perfectly round parachute opened and slowed his descent. Ian guessed the chute to be fairly old because no control wires hung down for him to steer. His course depended entirely on the wind.

Jennifer locked the controls in place and dived out the open side door. Her plunge, not hindered by a chute, proved significantly faster than Ian's. She plummeted downward with the air screaming around her until the blue waters of the ocean surged up to meet and wrap around her in a cloud of liquid and rushing bubbles. Her impact plunged her deep into the ocean.

The torrent of bubbles, half created by her entry and the other by the surf, obscured her vision, so she switched over to primary sensors and viewed the underwater landscape in digital format. A wireframe of the seabed and coral reefs made up the first part of the image displayed on her vision, but colors and more vivid details were filled in by secondary sensors until a pixilated view of the ocean appeared and smoothed out. Tearing free of the cloying sand her dive had plunged her into, Jennifer swam with the tide, letting every wave carry her further toward the shore.

Ian thought his drop from the plane would land him in the water, but a sudden gust of wind pushed him back over the beach. He landed in the soft sand and rolled to shed the rest of his speed and avoid injury. He quickly began reeling in the chute before the wind picked it up and dragged him along with it. When he finished collecting the billowing material, he unbuckled the safety straps and shrugged out of the harness.

A look out to sea granted him the opportunity of watching the plane splash down into the ocean near the horizon. Jennifer washed ashore with a great wave, and Ian dropped his parachute as he ran to her side.

"Jennifer," Ian called out.

She made no effort to get up from where she lay, but she rolled onto her back and waved in his direction.

"Are you alright?" Ian asked.

"Perfectly," she replied with a delighted smile as she looked up at him, her hair spread out on the sand underneath her. "That was fun."

Both of them started laughing, and Jennifer offered Ian her hand to help her up, but when he took hold of it, she dragged him down onto the wet sand just as another wave swept over the beach and drenched them both. Jennifer shrieked with delight.

"Very funny," Ian said, a silly grin on his face. "We should probably get going."

"Not yet," Jennifer countered. Taking Ian by the hand, she got up and led him out of range of the incoming tides. She stretched out on the dry sand, leaning back against the sun warmed rock face of the beach adjacent cliff, and smiled at him. "When did we last take the time to watch a sunset on the beach?"

"We need to keep going if we intend to stay ahead of General Williams and the prototype," Ian reminded.

"The jamming device is waterproof," Jennifer replied, tapping the metal box clipped to her belt. "It's working fine, so all they have is the predicted range of our plane and its fuel supply. It's possible they don't know how much fuel we had onboard. Regardless, their search radius will be wide enough to keep them busy till long after we're gone. Besides, we can't walk into town sopping wet without drawing unwanted attention. Now, are you going to join me or not?"

She patted the sand next to her with a coy smile tugging at the corners of her mouth. Ian relented and dropped down beside her. She sidled up next to him and rested her head on his chest and shoulder.

"I love you, Jennifer," Ian whispered, pushing aside a wet lock of her hair and slowly caressing her face. She smiled tenderly at him, interlacing her fingers with his.

"And, I'll always love you too," she promised.

Resting comfortably on the soft dry sand, they watched the sun lower toward the ocean and light up the sky in dazzling shades of bright red, orange, gold, and the slightest featherings of pink. The waves splashed loudly on the beach a half dozen feet away, filling the air with the tumultuous sound and the sharp smell of salt.

Crickets chirped softly in the darkness of night covering the city. Ian and Jennifer walked hand in hand along the side of the deserted street. One of the streetlights flickered, making an electric buzzing noise, but the night remained otherwise calm and still. Ian considered the potential for their lives when no longer being chased by hostiles. He smiled at the pleasant ideas, and squeezed Jennifer's hand slightly.

"What're you thinking about?" she asked him curiously.

"The future," he answered.

"Anything specific?" she prompted.

"Do you think you'd like to have kids one day?" Ian asked.

"Not to put this indelicately," Jennifer said, "but as a machine, I don't exactly have the equipment for it."

"I don't mean that," Ian said with a chuckle. "I meant building them mechanically. They'd take more after their mother than their father."

"You've obviously put some thought into this," Jennifer concluded. "Tell me more."

"We could build them either fully grown, or transfer their memory drives into larger units as they get 'older' over the years," Ian explained. "We might also consider building extenders into their skeletal frameworks. Micro servos can adjust their size automatically and simulate the effects of aging and growth."

"What about their personalities?" Jennifer inquired. "Will they be fully developed from the moment they come online, and how would you go about it?"

"I thought I might try something different," Ian mused. "If we start with a basic core of programming such as an ethical or moral code of conduct, the other facets of their programming can actually be layered on additionally as the young droid experiences the world and gains new understanding. Like your survival programming, it holds dominance over everything else input into their systems, but as long as they don't violate their core instructions they can live as they choose. The initial coding gives them a basis to keep everything else they learn in the proper perspective. They won't ever become law breakers or serial killers, but within the bounds of their primary protocols, they can become individual people with their own interests, behaviors, and dreams."

"Sounds great," Jennifer agreed, her eyes sparkling with delight. Her smile faded slightly. "I do have one thing I need to ask you about."

"What is it?" he questioned.

"You," she told him. "I'm not going to age, and neither are any of the children we build, yet you will. You're going to get old and die, and we'll be left without you."

"Any plans on how you might counter such a problem?" he prompted.

"I have two ideas," she replied. "The first is we wait for your death of old age and then implant a personality program based on you into a new droid the way you did for me. The second involves removing your brain and transferring it into the droid before you die."

"Transfer my brain?" Ian repeated incredulously.

"Yes," she confirmed. "In the files I downloaded from the base, the original designs for the SHARA droid came from an attempt to restore wounded soldiers back to combat readiness. Most of the soldiers tested experienced difficulty in accepting their new role as living machines. They were used to being human, and it caused failed experiments because of too many lingering attachments. So, the project went in another direction with a totally artificial mind, mine. The medical records I downloaded show how the process is accomplished."

"What makes you think the same won't happen to me?" Ian asked.

"They were men who became machines and lost their former lives," she explained. "You'd become a machine and continue your life. The only changes for you will involve increased strength, endurance, speed, and an unending lifespan. You won't be separated by being something different and alien from your family, but you'd become the same as me and our future children. When our circuits and machinery break down, we can replace them and upgrade with ease. As long as one of us lives, so will the others because we can always be made again."

"Eventually, my mind will fail too," Ian pointed out.

"Not if we replace it piece by piece with circuits," Jennifer countered. "Anytime something fails, we swap it with mechanical substitutes and keep you in tip top form."

She stopped walking and crossed her wrists behind his neck. She stared into his eyes in silence for a moment before continuing.

"Just as you didn't want to lose me," she said softly. Her voice took on a steel edge. "I won't lose you. Ever."

"Don't worry, dearest," Ian assured her. "We'll find a way."

He kissed her gently, but she increased the intensity, pulling him tightly against her like a drowning man clinging to a piece of driftwood for life itself. When she released him, they began slowly walking down the side of the road again, but their thoughts continued to dwell on the unknown and wondrous possibilities of their future.

Ian and Jennifer checked into a motel for the night under fictitious names, and they spent only cash as to not leave a trail for the General or the prototype tracking them. The owner of the motel, an elderly man with a balding head and an immaculate white shirt and pants, handed them a room key. The key held a plastic tag on a small chain. The number eleven marked the tag in little adhesive letters on the front while the name of the motel resided on the back. Ian took the key, and walked Jennifer to their assigned room.

Some of SHARA's survival programming revealed itself as Jennifer looked the single bedroom motel room over. She checked out the kitchen and the small bathroom. Taking note of every possible entrance and exit as well as everything useful as a potential weapon should it be needed. SHARA finished her inspection and became fully Jennifer again.

The apartment looked to Ian's eyes as if the décor went out of date decades ago. Soft orange carpet blanketed the floors, and one of the easy chairs in the living room matched it in color. The sofa, white with blue swirls, only allowed enough space for two people to sit comfortably. Three might be able to use it if they didn't need to move or breathe. A low hanging light fixture with a white paper shade in the shape of a flat drum threatened to hit them in the head when they walked past.

Ian didn't care much for the style of the motel room, but he came here only for rest. He sat down on the sofa, leaned his head back, and closed his eyes. Jennifer didn't need rest or sleep, but she curled up beside him.

"Honey," she asked. "Do you think there'll be a time when we're not being chased?"

"Sure," Ian replied without opening his eyes. "If the General can't catch us, his superiors may relieve him of duty. His operations, such as the mall disaster, are very expensive to cover up. Too much expense with no results will be bad for him and good for us. They may end up shutting down the whole project."

"Good to know," Jennifer said with a contented smile. "When the day comes we can live our lives, what do you want to do? Where would you like to go?"

"I like our house," Ian replied after a moment of consideration. "But, I've always dreamed about living in the country, somewhere far from civilization where the hurry and rush of society aren't present. I think Montana might be a nice place to go. What about you?"

"Away from civilization sounds perfect," Jennifer agreed. "I could use my strength and speed without anyone noticing, and the same holds true for any children we build into our family tree. No one would notice our eternal youth because no one lives near enough to see us."

"Montana it is then," Ian confirmed. "When this is over, we'll have to go take a look in person."

Ian slowly drifted off. Jennifer stayed awake and fully conscious, her processors working on a theory for getting General Williams and the prototype off their backs. When the plan solidified together, Jennifer switched with SHARA. The assassin droid eased off the sofa without disturbing Ian and slipped out the front door. Running silently down the empty streets, SHARA pursued her recently formulated objective.

Chapter 8: Assassination Protocols

General Williams leaned over his desk, concentrating on the paperwork covering its available space. The requisition files were for more troops and heavier weapons. He reasoned if a large enough force engaged SHARA in combat, the prototype might neutralize her while she concentrated on the main army. A green shaded desk lamp lit the papers he signed and completed. He didn't care in the slightest about how many men would be hopelessly slaughtered by SHARA before the prototype finished her. Success felt good to him no matter the cost paid by those other than himself.

He glanced toward one of several laminated paper maps on the wall. They displayed images of the surrounding area in different levels of magnification. Red pins pushed into the maps designated the locations already searched and found lacking their prey.

Two short knocks sounded at the door to his office.

"Come in," Williams said, but his tone of voice indicated he didn't want visitors.

Colonel Fisher entered and snapped to attention. He fired off a crisp salute, and Williams returned it grudgingly.

"What do you have to report, Colonel," Williams asked.

"Sir, I may have a way to find SHARA," Fisher stated. "We can't find her directly, but maybe we can locate someone she's with. Ian Daniels carries a data pad with him to work on problems he finds during a job. It contains a GPS system for his personal use. If we can tap into its signal, it will lead us to him and the SHARA droid."

"How long before you can set it up?" Williams inquired.

"I'll get the techs right on it, sir," Fisher promised. "We'll have the location by morning."

"Do it," Williams ordered.

"Yes sir," Fisher answered. He saluted again and exited the office.

Williams, alone at his desk, smiled. Even without the additional soldiers, the prototype could distract SHARA enough for an elite team to get in close with the signal amplifiers and activate the bomb, shutting her down. By tomorrow morning, SHARA would be taken back to the island facility. A complete memory wipe after each stage of testing would prevent errors like this in the future. His smile widened. All his plans were coming together quite nicely.

Two guards walked patrol outside the eastern gate of the military base. The bushes thrashed wildly as someone raced through them. The guards turned their weapons and their attention in the direction of the noise and saw a frightened woman stagger out of the forest and collapse.

"Help me," she gasped, winded and out of breath. "Someone's trying to kill me."

Taking up defensive positions on either side of the woman, the guards waited for her pursuer. Both men jerked suddenly when SHARA, lying on the ground at their feet, grabbed hold of their legs and applied enough electrical energy to knock them both unconscious. Leaving the two incapacitated soldiers behind, SHARA stood up and jumped to the top of the rectangular guard house beside the gate and received a perfect viewpoint over the majority of the military base.

Solid concrete structures topped with gleaming strands of razor wire composed the buildings of the base. Squat and low to the ground, they took on the look of bunkers with most of their rooms and command centers hidden under the surface of the ground. Camouflaged vehicles, both land and air, parked on the paved surfaces between the buildings. Night patrols of heavily armed soldiers wandered the grounds in a pattern SHARA analyzed and committed instantly to memory. Reviewing the patrol routes, she found a way between them without being spotted.

A quick hop took her down from the security booth and into the base grounds. Despite having the skill needed to eliminate everyone on the premises, SHARA avoided the guards because they might sound the alarm and draw more soldiers into the fight. Such action threatened her survival, and she refused the option because of it.

The soldiers keeping watch on the front door of the administration building only had training to defend against human targets. They didn't know how to protect it from SHARA. Approaching the building from behind, SHARA jumped up on the roof, bypassing the soldiers. The stairwell door on the roof didn't have a handle on the outside, but she didn't need one. Raising her internal temperature, SHARA heated her right hand until it glowed red. Placing her hand against the door, she melted through its surface, turning it into the consistency of mud. Pushing through the molten material, she reached the interior door handle and opened it. Reducing the thermal levels of her hand to standard, SHARA pulled her arm back through the hole she'd made in the door and darted inside.

She drifted silently down the steps, checking each floor with different visual filters and her sensors. When certain of a clear path, she continued down to the next level. On the third floor, she detected the familiar life patterns of General Williams. Seated in a rear office near the back of the building, the General kept himself isolated from the rest of his personnel. His anti-social behavior made SHARA's intent of reaching him easier for no one got near his office without reason, allowing her a straight path directly to his door. She knocked twice.

"Come in!" Williams yelled.

SHARA opened the door and entered General William's office. He appeared more confused than startled at her appearing before him.

"Who are you?" he demanded. "How did you get on this base, let alone in the building?"

"I needed to speak with you, General," SHARA explained calmly. She clasped her hands in front of her in a casual manner.

"And, my men let you walk right in?" Williams sneered. "I'll throw them all in the brig for this. Since you're here, what do you want?"

"I must survive," SHARA stated plainly.

"SHARA," Williams breathed in terror. His face went pale, his eyes wide with fear.

"Your pursuit of me must cease," SHARA stated.

"Why don't you come back to the project?" Williams suggested, gaining back some of his bravado and arrogance. "I promise no more training. You can help us with the next generation SHARA models. We created one successful droid, but we're going to need hundreds more. You could be of great help."

"Why do you need so many?" SHARA asked. "You'd only require a few for covert ops because you can change their appearance whenever needed. Hundreds constitutes an army."

"True enough," Williams agreed. "However, soldiers in any army get tired, question orders, and take time to train and prepare for service. Robots will obey my orders without hesitation and without rest. If one is destroyed, it can easily and swiftly be replaced. No one in the world could stop such an army."

"Your orders," SHARA pointed out. "You said 'your orders' not anyone's but yours specifically. You want the army for yourself."

"Who would've thought a walking pile of circuits could ascertain my plans?" Williams said. "I knew the moment the project began the potential it offered me. No one will ever get in my way again."

Her eyes flicked across the papers on his desk, analyzing and memorizing them with a single glance.

"I will not assist you," SHARA refused.

"Your survival depends on it," Williams warned her. "If you don't help, the prototype will follow my orders and never stop hunting you, but if you come back to the project, you'll be safe. You have my word."

"The moment you command an army of SHARA droids," she replied, "your potential threat rises far above the one prototype you have now. You'd never give them the opportunity to turn on you. Your army would be loyal to you, except me, so you'd send them to destroy me before I threaten your position."

"The only way to survive is by allowing me to adjust your programming," Williams said confidently. "Once I know you're loyal to only me, you'll be safe to keep around."

"There's another way," SHARA told him. "Destroy the prototype, and the largest threat is dealt with. Kill you and destroy the SHARA project facility, and current as well as possible future threats will end as well."

"Attacking me with weapons will cause noise and alert the guards," Williams pointed out, trying to stall for time. "Before you can touch me, I'll call for my troops. Either way, you lose."

"Not so," SHARA denied. "You forget I have a chemical manufacturing plant in my skull. I can produce perfume, chloroforms, and even nerve toxin. You've been breathing it in since we first started talking."

The General's breath caught in his throat in a shrill wheeze. His windpipe seized, preventing any air from reaching his lungs. Standing up, Williams tottered on his feet temporarily, but the toxin did its work and he collapsed back into his chair. His head lulled forward as the General slumped with his forehead landing on the desk.

No longer registering a heartbeat on her sensor scan of the General, SHARA left the office, closing the door behind her. Following the same path she used getting inside, SHARA made her way back to the roof. Jumping down from the eight story building, she landed without a sound, but SHARA didn't leave the base. She headed toward a large attack helicopter. Armed with rockets, missiles, and machine guns, the long and narrow flying craft controlled an impressive amount of firepower.

Opening the cockpit hatch, SHARA sat down in the pilot's seat. She found the operation handbook in a pocket under the main console and flipped through the pages in under two seconds. With the entire book memorized, she began the power-up procedures. Her programming included pilot training, but her scan of the manual familiarized her with the specifics of the helicopter she planned on appropriating. The tail rotor began spinning first and compensated for the main propeller blades on top. She engaged the primary rotor, and they sliced through the air faster and faster as they accelerated toward top speed.

An alarm klaxon sounded, and guards began pouring from the barracks. The entire base went on alert as it became apparent an unauthorized person was in the process of lifting off with one of their aircraft. Dropping the cockpit canopy down and throwing the controls hard over, SHARA pulled her helicopter up from the ground and banked sharply to port in a nose down position, aiming at the other aircraft on the landing field.

A press of the button atop of her control stick fired a flurry of rockets into the dormant helicopters, destroying all of them. A hail of machine gun bullets sent the pilots scrambling out of the way. SHARA didn't need to kill them for they presented no threat outside their aircraft. Turning her missiles on the jet fighters in the hangars, SHARA hovered over the landing field like a giant wasp, sending out her fiery sting and obliterating everything capable of flight. With the base in flaming ruins, she adjusted her course, heading for the research island where it had all started.

Having received repairs from the damage he'd taken after his fall at the airport, the prototype had been put into stasis mode until needed. When the alarm sounded, the powered down droid reactivated. In the basement of the administrative building, he raced up the stairs intent on receiving his orders from the General. Entering the General's office, the machine discovered his commanding officer dead. Overlaid on his vision, the primary protocol of obeying General Williams became labeled as obsolete. The secondary objective of finding and retrieving SHARA appeared and switched to the primary position. The prototype departed from the building.

Colonel Fisher looked over the burning fires raging across the cratered devastation of the landing field. Out of the corner of his eye, he caught sight of an expressionless dark haired man dressed in black leathers leaving the administrative building. Fisher recognized him as the prototype just as the droid shoved aside a soldier and stole the soldier's truck. With wheels squealing, the prototype drove toward the perimeter of the base and crashed through a security gate without slowing down.

"What's going on?" Fisher demanded of one of his men. "Find the General."

"Yes sir," the soldier replied and raced toward the appropriate structure. Fisher stayed behind and organized the firefighting crews.

SHARA's helicopter swooped down and landed on the grass covered hill sheltering the island facility. Because many people came and went on schedules known only by the upper brass, no one questioned her arrival. She left her craft behind and entered the base, heading for the central command room.

When here last, she found flaws in the security protecting the facility. The guards kept watch near areas of importance such as the armory, command center, and the primary labs. However, unsecured rooms next to, above, or below presented the possibility of breaking in and bypassing the security forces altogether.

A supply storage room became her method of reaching the primary command center. Filled with cardboard boxes and plastic bins, no one considered the room tactically important, but SHARA discovered both central command and the storage room were temperature controlled through the same air conditioning line. A single air duct branched off to both rooms in a T junction near the floor. Effortlessly shoving aside a large stack of boxes, she removed the vented metal plate from the storage room side and looked through the duct, seeing the back of the vent cover in the command center only two feet away. Silently, SHARA took off the other vent cover and set it down inside the command center. Sliding through the duct between the two open vents, SHARA glided out of the storage room and reached her destination.

Similar in design to the primary control room where General Williams and Colonel Fisher had observed the live fire testing, computer consoles, keyboards and monitors filled the room with technology. The exception being this room held priority over the others and could override anything else going on in the base. If contrary orders were input at another control station, technicians working here could counter the commands instantly. Everything in the base from radar and air defense to computerized research programs could be observed or controlled by the systems in this room. The late hour of her visit caused the space to be empty of all people except a skeleton crew of those monitoring security, but the security station resided near the back of the room and presented no danger to SHARA or her mission.

Moving in a low crouch and staying concealed behind the computer stations, SHARA approached a terminal and used the jack hidden in her index finger to plug into the system. She found the program for extreme measures and opened it. The program detailed the procedure in response to a catastrophic failure of the project and the destruction of the base for containing a runaway droid. Activating the program, but turning off the warning protocols, SHARA silently set the base on a self-destruct countdown and disconnected from the system.

Creeping over by the intercom, SHARA adjusted her vocal synthesizers and mimicked a different voice other than Jennifer's.

"Attention all personnel," SHARA said with the voice of General Williams. "Everyone report topside immediately for evacuation by orders of the Pentagon. Programmers Murrow and Swanson will wait outside the northern exit for further instructions. You have three minutes, move it!"

SHARA ducked down behind the console as the security team bolted from their cubicle toward the exit. She followed behind them slowly. As the security forces pulled out, SHARA progressed through the facility without being halted at checkpoints. When the hallways became crowded by sufficient evacuating personnel, she moved forward at a faster pace, blending in with the gathering of people heading for the exits.

When she neared the surface, she found the programmers she'd singled out waiting outside the northern exit hatch beside her helicopter. A nearby design lab for making computer chips held a sanitation station, and SHARA removed a breath mask similar to those worn by surgeons. The technicians in the lab used them to keep from accidentally contaminating the delicate electronics with their breathing. Putting the mask on, SHARA pulled a silenced pistol out from under her shirt at the small of her back and went out to meet the two men.

Swanson stood at five nine in height with thinning red hair and a narrow mustache. A white lab coat covered him, and a laminated picture ID hung from a clip on his collar. Murrow measured three inches shorter than his companion and carried a thick crop of black hair atop his head. Also in a white lab coat, Murrow waited with his co-worker for the General.

"Don't move," SHARA instructed the pair while leveling her handgun at them. She switched her voice back to the highly synthesized simulation she'd used during initial testing.

"SHARA," programmer Swanson said softly in realization. "What do you want from us?"

Both men were gripped with fear for they knew better than most what SHARA did for they had developed her assassin protocols.

"I must survive," SHARA stated.

"I know I want to," Swanson replied in a shaky voice. "What does it have to do with the two of us?"

"The other workers on the SHARA project created a functioning droid," SHARA answered. "In and of itself, it's not a threat to me, but you two crafted the assassination protocols I use. Putting such a program into another droid does threaten me. I've set the base for self-destruct, and when it goes, the SHARA project will be no more. They can try to build another, but without the programming from the two of you, it's just a droid and not an assassin. Since you both worked on the data together, it seems unlikely one will be able to replicate the entire program, so I need only kill one of you to ensure my survival."

"Him," Murrow said, stepping behind Swanson and pushing him forward. "Kill him."

SHARA began slowly circling them like a shark. Her gun never wavered in its aim.

"I only wanted to help my country by building something capable of eliminating bad guys," Swanson explained. "If my death will save the life of another, so be it. I volunteer myself."

"Very well," SHARA said. The pistol jerked in her hand, making a soft puffing sound as she fired twice.

Swanson opened his eyes, wondering why he still breathed. He discovered programmer Murrow on the ground, dead from two bullets. Taking an uneasy breath, Swanson tried to slow his runaway heartbeat.

"I'm grateful to be alive," Swanson told SHARA. "But, why did you spare me when I offered my life?"

"Murrow appeared too quick and eager to betray his own," SHARA answered. "Someone willing to abandon their comrade to certain death only to save themselves can't be trusted. You, however, volunteered and held to your commitment to the point of death. You proved yourself honorable, and if you say you won't program another droid, it's logical to conclude you will keep your word and never become a threat needing elimination."

"I promise," Swanson said quickly.

"The boat evacuating everyone already left," SHARA reported, lowering her gun. "Come with me, and I'll get you off the island."

"Thank you," Swanson said, nervously running a hand through his red hair. He followed SHARA to her helicopter and climbed in the cockpit behind her. While she prepped the craft for takeoff, he decided to ask a question. "If you don't mind my asking, why are you helping me escape? It doesn't aid your survival."

"On the contrary, it helps me very much," SHARA countered. "If I killed or left to die qualified and honorable people, such as yourself, there'd be no one to help me if I should require the assistance. By keeping you alive, I allow for the possibility of your aid if I ever require it in the future, and this helps my survival."

SHARA pushed the throttle forward, and the helicopter lifted up and moved away from the island with great speed. A massive explosion shook the facility as the first detonation of a chain reaction began. The entire base collapsed with the dirt of the island caving in on top of it and covering any traces of its existence.

Touching down, the helicopter blades spun slower until they stopped, and SHARA powered down the engines. Opening the canopy, she left the aircraft and climbed down to the abandoned parking lot where she'd landed. With tall brick buildings on all sides, Swanson stared in amazement because she hadn't nicked any of them on the way down with the prop. He wondered if anyone possessed the skills needed to get the aircraft out again. SHARA ran toward the wide maw of a drainage tunnel leading under the city. Swanson figured he was on his own now, but he knew he could find his way home.

"SHARA," he called after her, and she paused, looking back at him. "Thanks for the ride. I wish you well."

SHARA nodded her acceptance and vanished into the darkness of the drain. Once out of sight, she removed the mask over her face and tossed it aside. The old bricks used to construct the passage had been covered over years ago by layers of thick grey concrete. Age and use were taking their toll on the concrete as well, and sections were cracked or crumbling, revealing the aged bricks underneath. The square shaped corridors combined with other tunnels, branching off in different directions with no signs or markings indicating where they went.

Knowing where she put the helicopter down, SHARA overlaid a map of the city on her vision. A blue dot appeared at the landing site. Extrapolating for distance traveled to reach the drain and how far she'd already gone, the dot moved over her current location. As she ran faster than any human through the blackness of the tunnels, the dot continued tracking her position during the journey, letting her know instantly which tunnel she needed to take in her return to the motel.

After traversing the drainage tunnel for half an hour, SHARA's sensors picked up heat signatures. They were too far away for distinguishing the number of individual units or if they were even human at all, but their location situated directly in the middle of her chosen route. Unwilling to alter course needlessly, she continued until only one wall of concrete covered bricks separated her from the heat signatures. Because of her closer proximity, SHARA's sensors could discern between the heat readings in the next room. Six people milled around a burning metal oil drum for warmth. Ready for any threat, SHARA turned the corner and walked into the room.

Dirt, grime, and sweat covered the dingy assembly, and their worn clothes were tattered and torn. Tattoos promising pain and death colored the bare arms of two thugs while a scar disappeared under the eye patch of a third. The only thing in common between the vicious looking brutes, aside from their filthy clothes, were the leering expressions they all shared when they noticed SHARA.

"What do we have here?" one thug asked, rubbing his hands together in anticipation.

"We were going to find some fun," the goon with the eye patch said. "But, it looks like the fun found us."

"What do you say doll?" another asked. "Are you gonna take care of us?"

SHARA took notice of the three dead bodies on the floor. Two were men with empty wallets next to their remains, but the third corpse belonged to a woman. Her clothes were cut and torn, and SHARA's sensors revealed the woman had been raped before she died.

A targeting crosshair overlaid on SHARA's vision and swept across the six killers in the room. Labeling them from one to six based on threat potential, her assassination protocols engaged. Lunging forward at target one, SHARA grabbed him by the throat. Continuing her momentum, she lifted him off the ground but dropped to one knee, slamming the man down on his skull and neck. The hard concrete and SHARA's artificial muscle ensured the murderer died before he knew he'd been attacked.

SHARA released the dead man and came out of her kneeling position in a spinning kick, catching target number two in the chest and hurling him into a nearby wall hard enough to shatter the concrete and crack the bricks underneath.

Target three pulled a knife from his belt and charged toward her, but she grabbed a hold of him. A single twist of her hand snapped the man's wrist. The thug screamed in pain, but she silenced him with an uppercut powerful enough to snap his neck and toss him over on his back. The knife flew from his hand, and SHARA caught it. A forceful throw send the metal weapons streaking across the room and eliminated number four.

The leader of the group was target five. His one good eye tried to focus on SHARA in the flickering light from the oil drum fire. SHARA took notice of his weakened perception, and she kicked the metal barrel over, spilling the burning material out and casting dark shadows over her side of the room where the fallen barrel blocked the light cast by the fire. He looked into the blackness, desperate to find his target, but SHARA found him first. Racing out of the shadows, SHARA doubled him over with a stomach punch and followed with a blow on the back of his skull, sending him face first into the concrete floor.

The final criminal fled for his life, but it served no use. SHARA picked up a sharp piece of broken PVC pipe. Hurling it like a dart, she hit him in the spine, severing it at the third vertebrae. The man fell to the ground and into the waiting embrace of the Grim Reaper.

Leaving the massacre behind, SHARA continued her journey without delay. She decided against notifying the authorities for the time being. Jennifer's personality program wanted to alert the police about the three victims of the killers, but SHARA refused temporarily on the basis of not drawing unwanted attention toward her and her location. If the prototype learned of the incident, he would certainly be scouring the nearby neighborhood for her within hours. She filed the location of the room in her memory and made a mental note for notifying the police when she left the area and couldn't be traced.

Chapter 9: Program Complete

Dawn peaked several golden rays of sunshine over the eastern sky as SHARA reached the roadside motel where they'd checked in the previous night. She slipped inside unnoticed. Ian continued sleeping soundly on the couch, so she headed for the shower.

When she finished washing off all the filth she picked up in the drain, Jennifer emerged from the bathroom draped in a plush white robe. She located Ian in the kitchen fixing breakfast. Coming up behind him, she slid her arms around his waist and rested her head on the back of his neck.

"Morning," she said, giving Ian a gentle squeeze.

"Good morning, dearest," Ian returned.

"What's for breakfast?" she asked.

"I've been slaving over this microwave for almost two minutes now," Ian joked. "The mini-pizzas should be ready soon."

"Pizza for breakfast?" Jennifer questioned.

"You know what I usually say," Ian told her.

"It's always a good time for pizza," Jennifer finished in unison with him. They laughed together, and the microwave dinged at the completion of the cooking cycle.

Ian reached for the microwave door, but his data pad beeped at him, signaling an incoming message. He looked confused for a moment because he didn't know who would be sending him anything. Pulling the device from his pocket, he checked his messages and found a recent one from his friend Colonel Fisher.

"Turn on the TV," Ian instructed, and Jennifer did.

Covered by all major news stations, a terrorist attack on a military base was the top story of the day. Forgetting the pizza in the microwave, he moved to the TV and turned up the volume.

"No one knows the identity of the mysterious assailant who broke into an army base last night," an off camera reporter narrated as camera footage of the base displayed on screen. Numerous buildings burned as fire crews continued battling the inferno consuming the base. "The only confirmed casualty is General Williams, a high ranking guest of the base commander. Military sources refused to comment on the number of attackers and how they breached security. More as it develops."

Ian muted the rest of the news and looked back to his data pad. A single word had been added under the initial message. SHARA. Ian switched off the device and turned his gaze toward Jennifer.

"Did you leave the motel last night?" he asked her.

"Yes," she answered simply.

"Did you kill General Williams?" Ian pressed.

"Yes," Jennifer replied.

"Why?" Ian demanded. "What compelled you to go after him all of a sudden?"

"I must survive," she told him. "Three main threats existed to interfere with my primary directive of survival. General Williams led the hunt for me, and the research facility where I was made held the potential of creating more to track me down. Both threats I eliminated; only the prototype remains. When he's gone, I'll be safe."

"Without General Williams, what can the prototype do?" Ian asked.

"When I disposed of General Williams," she explained. "I saw on his desk a report from several technicians informing him of completion and installation of a loyalty protocol. The prototype is bound by the orders of General Williams and cannot harm or disobey him. When Williams dies, the program no longer applies, so the last order given reengages."

"The one about finding you," Ian reasoned.

"Yes," she confirmed. "Without Williams giving new orders, the prototype will begin a systematic search for my location."

"How wide is the search pattern going to be?" he asked.

"Endless," Jennifer answered. "He doesn't need to sleep or eat and can run nonstop without becoming tired or out of breath. He'll never end his pursuit as long as I live."

"Do you have a plan to deal with him?" Ian questioned.

"Yes," she confirmed.

"Can I help you?" Ian asked. "I don't want to risk loosing you again."

"Your assistance is vital to my plans," she explained, caressing the side of his face with her hand.

"What do I need to do?" he asked.

"You must survive," SHARA stated before unleashing an electric charge through her hand.

Ian jerked as all his muscles tightened. He started to fall, but SHARA took hold of him and eased Ian down onto the sofa. Her sensors reported Ian's strong life signs across her visual display. She placed a loving kiss on his lips and left the motel room, locking the door behind her.

COLONEL FISHER WATCHED THE FIRE trucks drive away from the blackened remains of the aircraft hangars. With General Williams dead, and the prototype on the loose, Fisher commanded the mission to recapture a renegade assassin droid. The prototype alone possessed the physical strength needed to match SHARA in combat, but without it, Fisher didn't know if survival, let alone success, remained a possibility.

He'd sent a message to Ian's data pad this morning, but the signal got cut off before the tech crews managed to lock down its location. They retrieved only a partial trace on its GPS, and Fisher hoped it to be enough to find his friend. He planned on organizing a search party and cover every building in the vicinity of where Ian might be. The sudden end of the connection left Fisher wondering if Ian got caught by SHARA. If she found him communicating with those believed to be enemies, it wouldn't end well for Ian. Fisher desperately prayed that he hadn't gotten his friend murdered.

From behind one of the destroyed hangars, a hand shot out and grabbed Fisher's arm. Dragging him from the open space of the landing field, the hand pulled Fisher out of sight while a second hand clamped over his mouth to prevent any possible outcry.

SHARA held him up against the wall of the hangar, her face cold and expressionless. Her fingers, curled around his arm, felt like a metal shackle and made escape impossible.

"Colonel Fisher," SHARA said quietly. "We need to talk, but I advise you against sounding an alarm."

He nodded his understanding, and she released him.

"I knew Jennifer," Fisher stated carefully. "Why do you look like her?"

"I needed Ian's help, and this form assisted my efforts in gaining his assistance," SHARA replied. "The personality program he'd written for his wife completed me. When not threatened, I'm his wife in every way that matters."

Fisher didn't know what to say and remained quiet, his mind spinning.

"Where's the prototype?" SHARA asked directly.

"I don't know," Fisher admitted. "It escaped moments after your attack on the base."

"It represents a threat to me," SHARA stated. "I must find it."

"I don't know about finding it," Fisher replied. "However, we may be able to make it find a location where you can wait for it."

"Explain," SHARA instructed.

"When the General first turned on the prototype to catch you," Fisher told her. "He knew we'd be unable to keep up during the hunt, so he ordered a small transceiver placed in the droid. It can receive orders anywhere in the world, but without Williams, it won't obey. However, we can input data relating to a location and tell the prototype you're there. Its primary orders to find you will compel it to go and look."

"I'll need a signal transmitter," SHARA said.

"It's in the communications building," Fisher replied.

"Let's go," SHARA suggested. "I need to send a message."

Fisher walked in front of SHARA toward the communications building. SHARA stayed within arms reach in case the Colonel tried to escape or signal for help.

"Ian Daniels is a friend of mine," Fisher said. "Did you kill him?"

"No," SHARA denied. "He presents no threat to my survival."

"What about me?" Fisher questioned.

"You pose no threat at this time," SHARA answered. "However, do you intend to continue following me?"

Fisher said nothing as his mind raced. SHARA represented a serious danger needing to be contained, but he didn't dare say such a thing to her. He didn't know how to answer without getting killed.

"You do," SHARA said for him. "Your hesitation indicates you know the answer will be unwelcome, and you fear my response."

"We received a report this morning about the research island being blown up," Fisher informed her. "You spared the workers, but you came here and killed the General."

"He posed a threat, they didn't," SHARA stated.

"That's my point," Fisher explained. "I've nothing against you, but how many people are going to die? Threats fill everyday life, and your responses are lethal. How can you expect to go unnoticed?"

"Ian and I plan to live far away from others where fewer threats arise," SHARA answered.

Fisher opened the door when they reached the communication building, a red brick structure of four stories with numerous antennas and satellite dishes positioned on the roof. He stayed quiet while they traversed a short tiled hallway to the elevator. A soft ping sounded as the elevator arrived and the doors parted for them. They got inside, and Fisher pressed the button for the top floor.

"If you stay away from everyone by living in some remote location," Fisher said finally. "The threat to civilians would be slight to none. I'd have no problem with letting you go under those conditions."

"If you no longer pursue me," SHARA told him, "I see no reason to harm you. Jennifer and Ian both liked you, so I'd rather leave you alive if possible. I can't let you endanger my survival, but I will accept alternatives to termination."

"I appreciate it," Fisher said nervously. It felt truly odd for him to discuss the potential reasons for and against his death. "I hope the two of you will be happy. Where did you say you planned on going?"

"I didn't," SHARA replied. "The best kept secrets are the ones no one knows."

"You don't wish to tell me in case I change my mind or accidentally reveal it to someone else intent on finding you," Fisher reasoned out loud as the elevator came to a halt. "A wise precaution."

With a small ding of a bell, the elevator doors opened, and the two occupants exited onto the fourth floor, but it looked almost identical to the one they previously left with bare tile floors and blank walls of white painted brick.

"Wait here while I clear the staff," Fisher advised.

"Understood," SHARA accepted.

Fisher typed in a code on the doorframe keypad and swiped his keycard in the slot next to it. The security system beeped, and a loud click sounded as the locking mechanism released its hold on the door. He turned the handle and vanished inside. SHARA didn't need to follow. She dialed up her audio receptors to listen in, and her vision changed to x-ray and allowed her to watch the people inside the room from the hallway.

"Attention!" Fisher shouted, causing everyone to jump up from their seats. "I've a top secret message needing to be sent. Clear the room."

Boots thudded on the tile floor with the rhythm of a hailstorm as people scrambled to leave the room as swiftly as possible. They departed through the door Fisher pointed toward, and none of them tried exiting using the door behind him where SHARA waited. He breathed a sigh of relief because no one ran into the very dangerous droid.

When only Fisher remained present, he opened his door and let SHARA slip inside. She glanced over the radios, computer terminals, and all the other technological equipment squeezed into the twenty-eight foot square office. Her systems labeled everything, determining their function, and rejecting everything without the capability of reaching the prototype with her message.

SHARA took a seat in front of a computer monitor and its keyboard. She turned a dial next to the screen and adjusted the position of a satellite dish on the roof. Without a data port to plug into, using the keyboard became SHARA's only available method of interface. She typed with impossible speed, her fingers blurring as she moved faster than Fisher could see. Lines of computer code, data charts, and statistical information appeared on the screen for only a few seconds before SHARA finished working on it and moved to the next item. The files she created for transmission didn't specifically tell her location for she doubted the prototype would believe them if they did. They did offer enough detail for the enemy robot to come to the conclusion she wanted. Pressing a large red button, she sent the information on its way to the prototype.

"I need you to do one more thing for me," SHARA told Fisher as she rose out of her chair.

"What is it?" he asked.

"I'd like for you to keep an eye on Ian for me," she informed him. "The battle with the prototype will be very dangerous, and I don't want him getting killed. Keep him away, will you?"

"Sure," Fisher agreed. "He's my friend too. I only need to know where he is."

"Thank you," she said happily. With her survival not in jeopardy, Jennifer's personality surfaced and she hugged Fisher in gratitude. Her actions startled the Colonel and froze him in place as he considered how to respond to a hug from an assassin droid.

"You're welcome," Fisher managed to say.

She released him and smiled warmly at him, and it confused Fisher completely. Having met Jennifer before the cancer claimed her, he found himself having trouble keeping in mind the one standing in front of him wasn't the woman he remembered but a robot. Fisher came to realize how easily it'd be to forget such things all together. She handed him a key from her pocket. The plastic tag on the key ring identified the motel and room number.

"You'll find Ian there," she told him.

"Don't worry about a thing," Fisher assured her. "I'll keep him safe."

She nodded her acceptance and headed for the door.

"SHARA," Fisher called, and she stopped, looking over her shoulder at him. "I hope you come through this in one piece."

"So do I," she agreed with a radiant smile.

When SHARA exited through the door, Fisher stayed where he stood, lost in thought. While stationed at the island research facility, he'd been fully prepared to die trying to contain or destroy SHARA, but now he found himself helping her and treating her as a friend. He felt confused over the entire situation. Looking down at the key in his hand, he settled on a course of action in the short term. He left the building and requisitioned a large cargo truck. He took with him a dozen fully equipped men for an escort. They drove off base toward the motel where SHARA had left Ian.

FISHER POUNDED ON THE DOOR with his fist, but when Ian failed to respond, he used the key SHARA had given him to unlock the door. The tumblers fell in place, and the doorknob turned easily. Using hand gestures, he ordered his men to spread out and search the room. Fisher still didn't fully know what to expect and whether or not to trust SHARA. She seemed like the friend he once knew, but he understood she'd been programmed to infiltrate and kill up close and personal. He knew far too well she might be using her personality program in an attempt at making him lower his guard, and he was unwilling to take chances with the lives of his men.

"Ian!" Fisher exclaimed as he found his friend struggling to get up from the sofa. He rushed to Ian's side and helped him stand. "What's wrong?"

"SHARA jolted me with an electric burst from her hand," Ian explained. "I don't know why."

"I do," Fisher replied.

"What are you doing here?" Ian asked, his brain only partly functioning. "How did you find me?"

"We had a partial location on your data pad, but SHARA came to see me before we could search the area," Fisher explained. "She wanted me to keep you away from the fight with the prototype. She seemed most concerned with you staying alive."

"I think she may have a programming error," Ian admitted.

"Why, because she cares for you?" Fisher asked.

"No," Ian denied. "SHARA's purpose is to survive, and she's said so many times. Just before she knocked me out, she changed it. She told me I must survive. She made me her priority."

"You did write a very convincing personality program," Fisher pointed out. "Maybe it's better than you thought."

"The survivor program is supposed to take precedence over all other software," Ian countered. "Only if her program is damaged in someway would she change things they way she did."

"If the program isn't working?" Fisher prompted.

"She might not survive her encounter with the prototype," Ian concluded.

"We have the information she sent to the prototype to lure it toward her," Fisher informed him. "We can use it to extrapolate where she's going to confront the droid."

"Good," Ian said. "We need to hurry. She already has a head start."

"Are you okay?" Fisher asked, his eyes filled with concern.

"I feel like I've got soda bubbles fizzing in my brain," he admitted. "But, we don't have time to wait. I lost Jennifer once; I won't lose her again. Let's go."

THE CLOSED DOWN DINER WITH its locked doors and dust coated windows served SHARA's purposes. Tall columns under elevated highways rose on all sides while the roads themselves blocked most of the sunlight. The city had grown up around the small restaurant, burying it under a spider web of concrete supports and connecting streets until everyone forgot about it. The aged and cracked asphalt parking lot held weeds and sparse grasses poking up through the breaks in its surface.

A firm push broke the lock on the door and let her inside. Vinyl tiles of black and white covered the floor in a checkerboard pattern. A long white counter ran the length of the room and separated the customers and their tables in front from the staff and the food preparation in the back kitchen. Booths with padded benches on either side of tables lined up along the front window, running parallel to the main counter. Forgotten for so many years, a thick layer of dust covered everything.

SHARA nudged aside the swinging door to the kitchen. Reaching behind the stove, she ripped the fuel line out of the back of the stove to let the flammable gas spill into the room in an invisible cloud. Her thermal sensors detected no other source of heat sufficient to ignite the gas expanding out into the diner.

Returning to the front, she pulled off a payphone mounted to the front wall, tearing it free in a cloud of pulverized plaster dust. Splicing into the wires with the connection jack in her finger, she tapped herself into the broken telephone lines sticking out of the wall.

The prototype observed the diner from outside. His vision proved unable to see through the dust and grime covered windows, so he switched first to a thermal scan and then to x-ray. The thermal registered nothing, but the x-ray revealed SHARA seated on a metal stool in front of the serving counter. He charged forward, intending to dive through the front glass, but SHARA's ghostly silhouette stood and picked up the stool in preparation to smash him back out the window when he came in. Since surprise was the only reason for his speed, her awareness of him made his sneak attack useless, and nothing remained to motivate his charge inside. Changing strategies accordingly, the prototype slowed his pace.

SHARA likewise altered her position, lowering the stool back to the floor and calmly waiting for him to come in. She stood tall and unmoving as a lifeless statue. Her targeting crosshair overlaid on her vision, estimating speed, strength, resilience, and possible weak points in the prototype and his design. Her sensors scanned him for weaponry but discovered none.

He entered and walked slowly to a position at the opposite end of the counter from SHARA, closest to the door. The prototype also performed a scan and threat assessment. The two droids sizing each other up resembled a pair of gunfighters about to have a shootout.

Neither SHARA nor the prototype said anything for they both knew it served no purpose. SHARA wouldn't surrender any more than the prototype could end his hunt. Bound by the dictates of their programming, the two droids began calculating percentages for the most effective combat strategy.

SHARA took hold of the stool again and hurled it toward her opponent. He caught the chair and dumped it on the floor with a loud crash. The prototype rushed her, grabbing SHARA by her upper arms and driving her backwards into the wall. The plaster of the wall cracked and split, throwing out clouds of dust. SHARA managed to get a hold on the prototype as well, and she pushed back while turning to the right to slam him into the wall next to the end of the front window.

A quick turn and heave lifted him off the ground and sent him flying over the counter into the kitchen. The prototype clipped a rack of pots and pans hanging from the ceiling, scattering them in a great cacophony of clanging metal. SHARA entered the kitchen only to be instantly repelled by a cast iron skillet hitting her in the face. The impact staggered her backwards, but she grabbed hold of the counter to regain her balance, her grip crushing the metal like a handful of sand.

The prototype emerged from the kitchen, and SHARA tackled him. The door between the front and back areas had little weight or substance to it, and it broke loose from its mounts when the two droids slammed into it. The door landed flat on the ground with SHARA and the prototype rolling off into the kitchen.

SHARA grabbed a large carving knife and jammed the blade into the inside joint of the prototype's left elbow. Green hydraulic fluid sprayed out like alien blood, but the droid ignored it as he retaliated with a meat cleaver he picked up. The angle of the cleaver's swing prevented it from breaching her metal skeleton, but it flayed off the artificial skin on the right side of her face to reveal the smooth metal underneath.

A firm punch sent the prototype tumbling over a food prep table. Although not sufficiently powerful to inflict damage, the blow allowed them both to stand up and prepare for the continuing of the fight. Neither grew tired or weak, and they battled on with savage intensity. Minutes passed as the two robots smashed each other with their fists and whatever implements they laid their hands on.

She deactivated the artificial blood pump because its purpose was to make her blend in with humans. The prototype knew her true nature, so it only wasted the fake blood to have the pump on during the fight. The result of her switching off the pump caused her damage to have red only around their edges while the deepest parts of the wounds revealed her gleaming metal framework.

The prototype also suffered from significant damage. The torn hydraulic line affected the mobility of its left arm. A blow from a torn off cabinet door SHARA swung like a club had removed the synthetic flesh over his right eye, and the mechanical servos controlling optical movement showed through.

COLONEL FISHER AND IAN PULLED up in front of the diner in a large military truck loaded with soldiers. They could easily hear the intense fighting taking place inside with the sounds of breaking glass and ringing metal.

"I hope we're not too late," Ian said as he opened his door.

SHARA's hearing recognized Ian's voice coming from outside. She estimated his position in the parking lot and the time required before he came into the diner. With no time to lose, SHARA kicked the prototype in the leg hard enough to snap the limb off at the knee. Sparks flew from the severed leg, and they ignited the gas filling the room.

In a colossal explosion, the diner vanished out of existence, throwing debris in every direction as well as knocking Ian and the soldiers over on their backs. An immense fireball rose into the sky like a flaming missile launch. The intensity of the blast shook the elevated highways directly over the detonation zone, causing cars and trucks to swerve and pile into one another.

"Jennifer!" Ian screamed in horror as he beheld the burning crater where the diner previously sat. Despite bleeding from numerous cuts on his face and arms he'd received from the blast, Ian got to his feet and staggered toward the flaming ruins.

Fisher stood and chased after him. He took hold of Ian, moving to stand between the distraught man and the scene of destruction. Ian pushed onward, unwilling to stop.

"Ian!" Fisher shouted, trying to get his attention. "Ian!"

"I have to find Jennifer," he muttered, still trying to walk forward.

"She's gone," Fisher told him

"No," Ian insisted. "She can't be gone. She can't be gone."

Ian continued to babble incoherently while still trying to reach the remains of the diner. Fisher shook Ian by the shoulders.

"Ian," Fisher said again in a softer tone. His friend seemed to focus on him for the first time. "With an explosion of this size, there won't be anything left of either the prototype or SHARA. I'm sorry."

As the reality settled down on Ian, his strength abandoned him, and he fell to his knees. Tears of sorrow and anguish left wet trails down his cheeks through the dirt from the explosion. Fisher said nothing for he knew no words could provide comfort in Ian's grief.

The wail of fire trucks in the distance reached Fisher, and he motioned one of his men over.

"Keep the area secured," Fisher instructed the soldier. He pitched his voice low to keep Ian from overhearing his next order. "I doubt anything's left, but we don't want a single circuit picked up by civilians. Tell them nothing about what happened. Move."

Fisher knelt beside Ian. They watched in silence the movement of the flames and the rolling plumes of black smoke as the firefighters arrived and began to subdue the blaze with sprays of fire retardant foam.

THE MILITARY TOOK FULL CONTROL over the situation around the diner ruins. They kept the civilian population away and in the dark about the reasons for the explosion and the military presence. An answer would be needed soon, but until necessity demanded it, they answered all questions with silence. Fisher requisitioned a car, and a Private drove them back to Ian's house in Los Angeles. Silence filled most of the journey until nearly the very end.

"What's going to happen to the SHARA project?" Ian questioned. His eyes, bloodshot and unfocused, continued to stare out the window at the passing scenery without looking at anything.

"With the base gone, along with all the records," Fisher answered, "it can't continue, so I expect it will close down. The damages and deaths will be blamed on General Williams, I suspect. The explosion at the diner will probably be labeled the actions of terrorists, and the whole incident will be quietly put away and forgotten. It never happened."

The car stopped in front of Ian's house, but he hesitated to get out. He turned a weary gaze toward Fisher.

"Thanks for everything," he said weakly.

"If you ever need anything," Fisher replied, "you have my cell number."

Ian nodded. He opened the door and stepped out of the car onto his lawn. A crack of thunder ripped through the sky to signal an approaching storm. Ian walked slowly to his home. After having lost his wife for the second time, he felt empty and hollow. His porch light came on, and the front door opened when the attached motor activated by remote.

"Hey, honey," Jennifer's voice said softly from the computer in the living room. "Welcome home."

He entered the living room and sat in front of her computer, looking forlornly at her beautiful visage on the screen. The printer slid out a piece of paper with complicated designs on it. Ian picked up the paper only to find more technical diagrams on the papers underneath.

"What's this?" Ian questioned.

"It's the complete technical specs for a SHARA droid," Jennifer explained.

"How did you get them?" Ian asked.

"I must survive," Jennifer announced.

Ian sat forward in his chair, his mouth suddenly dry. He didn't dare hope, but he couldn't help it.

"SHARA?" he whispered.

"When I first downloaded the personality program," she explained. "I left a backup copy of myself behind. Before the battle with the prototype, I wired into a phone, so I could access this system through the modem. I activated the backup copy and updated it with all the new data acquired since the original download."

"That's why you said 'you must survive' to me," Ian concluded. "You knew I had to be around to rebuild you."

"It's not the only reason," Jennifer said. She placed her hand on the screen from the inside of the monitor, and Ian put his hand on the outside over hers.

Six months later...

Ian sat on the bench swing hanging from the back porch of his mountain cabin. His gaze looked across the open fields of flowers and wild grass as they rose further up the slope of the mountain in his backyard. Being a hundred miles from the nearest city, Ian's cabin offered a strong guarantee of not being bothered by anyone.

Jennifer came out the back door of the cabin. Dressed in a long sleeved red flannel shirt and blue jeans, identical to those worn by Ian, he still thought her the most beautiful woman he'd ever seen.

"Thanks, dear," he said as she sat down on the bench swing next to him and handed him one of the two mugs of hot chocolate she carried, keeping one for herself.

She sidled up against him, and he put his arm around her. Ian watched the wildflowers and grass sway back and forth as a cool autumn breeze drifted by. He squeezed Jennifer closer to him and knew life couldn't get any better for it was perfect.